JANE JEFFRY

JILL CHURCHILL

A KNIFE TO REMEMBER

A JANE JEFFRY MYSTERY

AVON
TWILIGHT

AVON BOOKS, INC.
1350 Avenue of the Americas
New York, New York 10019

Copyright © 1994 by The Janice Young Brooks Trust
Inside cover author photo by Stephen Locke Portraits
Published by arrangement with the author
Library of Congress Catalog Card Number: 94-94318
ISBN: 0-380-77381-3
www.avonbooks.com/twilight

First Avon Twilight Printing: March 1999
First Avon Books Printing: November 1994

AVON TWILIGHT TRADEMARK REG. U.S. PAT. OFF. AND IN OTHER COUNTRIES, MARCA REGISTRADA, HECHO EN U.S.A.

Printed in the U.S.A.

WCD 10 9 8 7 6 5

Jane Jeffry threaded through all the parked cars on
her street and pulled into her driveway, going very
slowly and carefully to avoid falling into the pothole
that was threatening to eat the whole driveway. She'd
investigated the costs of a new driveway and decided
the pothole would have to eat the whole block before
she could afford such an extravagance.

"Wow!" she said to herself, staring at the sight
of a large truck easing its way between her house
and her neighbor Shelley's.

Shelley herself was standing on the little deck
outside her kitchen door, likewise observing the
strange phenomenon and looking ready and capable
of stringing up the driver if he scraped her house.
Jane pulled her ailing and ancient station wagon
into her garage and went to join Shelley.

"Who'd have thought they'd start so early in the
day?" Jane said.

"And be so efficient!" Shelley said. "Jane, you
should have seen them take out the fence between
our yards. They popped the posts out like a line of
clothespins. And they've already got the dog runs
set up."

"Which Willard will probably be terrified of. What's that particular truck for?"

"I don't know."

Jane shivered. It was only the first Tuesday in October, but there was a chill in the air and the station wagon's heater had refused to work while she was driving her car pool. One more thing to start budgeting for! "Let's go inside and watch from my back windows. Uh-oh," she added as the big battleship gray Lincoln wallowed into her driveway behind them.

There was a nasty, scraping sound as the Lincoln fell into the pothole.

Cringing, Jane called out, "Hi, Thelma," as her mother-in-law, frowning furiously, emerged from the car.

"*Jane!* What's happened here?"

"I'm outta here," Shelley murmured.

Jane grabbed her friend's sleeve. "Don't you dare desert me," she hissed. Then, dragging Shelley along, she headed for her own house. "Thelma, come in out of the cold!"

Thelma was still sputtering with vicarious indignation when they got into the kitchen. "They're tearing up your whole yard! What happened to your fence? Have you called city hall?"

"Thelma, it's all right," Jane assured the older woman, pouring each of them a cup of coffee. "They're making a movie."

Thelma scoffed. "In your backyard? Come now, Jane!"

Jane set the cups, along with cream and sugar on a tray and led the way to the living room, where the large back windows overlooked the scene of chaos behind the house. "Not in our yards, in the field behind us. They're using our backyards for the equipment."

"That terrible field!" Thelma sniffed. "I've always said that was dangerous, all that open land."

"I know you've said that," Jane responded. *Almost every time you come here*, she added mentally. "But we like the field, don't we, Shelley? I'm glad the land developer went bankrupt before the division was finished and left that vacant land."

Thelma had seated herself with her back to the window, but curiosity overcame her and she set her coffee aside to get up and look outside. "But a movie . . . why would somebody make a movie here, of all places?"

"It isn't a whole movie," Shelley said. "Just a few scenes. They'll only be here a few days. And they're paying the homeowners very generously and installing brand-new fences for us when they're done."

She caught herself and gave Jane a quick, chagrined look as if to say, *Why am I apologizing?*

"Well, I think it's outrageous, disturbing your lives this way, just to make another film. Probably more of that Hollywood trash, anyway. There aren't enough good movies being made anymore."

While Thelma Jeffry finished her coffee, she continued to rumble about how the world had gone to the dogs, and things weren't like that in *her* day, and how she feared for the next generation. She finished up her tirade with a bit about Madonna's sex book, on which she seemed curiously well informed. Eventually she got to the point of the visit.

"I just dropped by to bring you your check, Jane. I'd best be on my way. I'm giving a talk at my club luncheon today and I need to refresh myself on my notes." She shrugged into her suit jacket and fished a large green check out of her purse to hand to Jane.

Jane's late (and progressively less lamented) husband Steve had been a partner in the Jeffry family's small chain of drugstores—along with his widowed mother and his brother Ted. In the early years of Jane and Steve's marriage, the business had hit a rough financial spot at about the same time as Jane received a tidy little inheritance from a great-aunt. She had put her money into the pharmacy. Because of her investment at a crucial time and her role as a partner's widow, Jane received a third share of the chain's monthly profits and always would.

Jane was entitled to the money, but Thelma always presented the check in person, and always managed to make it seem like charity on her part instead of Jane's due. And when possible, like today, she made the "gift" in view of witnesses.

Jane folded the check, ostentatiously *not* looking at the amount, and put it in her jeans pocket. "Thanks, Thelma," she said through nearly gritted teeth.

"Why do you let her do that?" Shelley asked when Thelma had finally gone.

"Because I'm a wimp!" Jane said. "I keep trying to see it from her viewpoint. Steve's been dead for almost two years now and is going to keep on being dead, if you know what I mean. He's not working for the pharmacies anymore and never will again. She probably resents having to give me a third, just as if he were still contributing to making the profits."

Jane let her big shambling dog Willard out of the basement, where he'd been hiding from Thelma, and the women went back to the living room and dragged a pair of armchairs nearer the window to watch what was going on outside. The big truck they'd watched pull in was now unloading its cargo. A huge sturdy yellow tent was being set up in Jane's yard and a similar tent in light green was going up in Shelley's yard. Another enormous flatbed truck had pulled into the field and big flat building components were being unloaded. Sham buildings were springing up before their very eyes and workers swarmed everywhere.

"I take it you haven't yet told Thelma about your trip with Mel this weekend," Shelley said, without looking away from the astonishing sight.

"God, no! I know I'm going to have to, but I just can't face it. I thought maybe Thursday."

"Uh-huh. You figure she won't have time to call out the National Guard to throw up a cordon around your house before Friday morning?"

"Something like that."

"So, when you *do* tell her, what are you going to say?"

Jane cleared her throat and gave it a practice run. " 'Thelma, you remember Detective Van Dyne, don't you? Well, I wanted to let you know he and I are going to New York for the weekend. I'm leaving Mike in charge of Katie and Todd and he'll have a number where I can be reached if there's any emergency. Good-bye.' Then I hang up real fast before she can say anything."

"And she'll call you back a millisecond later to read you the riot act."

"I'm ready for it. I'll just explain that I'm nearly forty years old, a competent adult widow, entitled to make these decisions myself. My oldest son is a senior in high school, a responsible boy who will look after his brother and sister. And then when she calls me a slut, I'll hang up on her again."

Shelley nodded. "Sounds good to me. You think she really is going to hit the roof?"

"Oh, I'm sure of it. I think she's always resented the fact that I didn't throw myself into Steve's grave. The idea that I might have a sex life will make her head spin." Jane paused. "Actually, it makes my head spin. Want a cookie? I made some to leave with the kids."

"Sure . . . they're not those tooth-breakers again, are they?"

"Shelley, you know that was just a mistake I made by not following the recipe closely enough."

Jane returned a minute later with some sugar cookies tinted pink and cut in the shape of hearts. Willard was so hard on her heels that he was nearly treading on her shoes.

"Too cute," Shelley said, taking a cookie and holding it well out of Willard's range. Willard sat down by Jane and looked at her adoringly.

"Have you told the kids your plans yet?" Shelley asked.

"Only Mike. He took it very well. I knew he would. Shelley, I don't know what I'll do without him when he goes to college next year. I think Todd will be okay about it, too. It probably won't occur to him that this is anything more than an adult sleepover. But Katie—"

Shelley was still gazing out the window as Jane spoke. She interrupted Jane's tale of maternal woe. "I think you're about to have company."

Jane gave Willard the last of her cookie and went to look. A woman in jeans and a padded, hooded jacket was in the yard where the large tent was almost set up. She was gesturing to a young man as she headed for Jane's back door.

Jane had the door open before the woman reached it. "Can I help you?" she asked.

The woman shoved back her hood with one hand and extended the other to Jane. "Hi. I'm Maisie Valkenberg. May I come in? I need to murder somebody!"

——— 2 ———

"Who's that?" Shelley asked as Jane came back into the living room.

"Somebody who needed to use the phone," Jane said, then fell silent as the two of them shamelessly eavesdropped on the half of the conversation going on in the kitchen.

"Listen, Anita," Maisie Valkenberg was saying firmly, "somebody's really fallen down on the job. The phone line isn't installed and I'm having to impose on the neighbors. My medical kit did *not* come out on Harry's truck like you promised me it would and I've already had a grip with a bad splinter. I had to borrow tweezers and peroxide from makeup. This is not the way to run things and I'm going to be talking to the producers in a few minutes. You don't want me unhappy, Anita. I can raise a really big stink if I need to. Safety regulations scare the money people half to death, you know."

There was a moment's silence, presumably while the downtrodden Anita tried to defend herself. Maisie briskly fired another barrage of threats at her before hanging up.

"Take notes, Jane," Shelley said in an undertone. "You might try that technique on Thelma."

"I'm really sorry to have bothered you this way," the visitor said, peeking her head in the living room door.

"It's no bother at all," Jane said. "Do you have a minute to sit down? You look like you could use something hot to drink. Coffee? Tea?"

"Oh, what a good, good woman you are!" Maisie exclaimed. "Coffee, please. As hot as you can make it. Craft services aren't set up yet either."

Jane and Shelley exchanged bewildered looks. "What does that mean?" Jane asked.

Maisie had come into the living room and was methodically stripping off layers of clothing: her padded jacket, mittens, a muffler, stocking cap, cable-knit sweater. A trim, pretty woman of about forty-five, with springy dark hair, flashing eyes, and a red turtleneck over jeans emerged from the extra clothes.

"I'm sorry. Craft services is the snack area in movie-ese. That's what's going into your backyard here. I really do apologize for bursting in here so rudely. I didn't even ask your name."

"I'm Jane Jeffry and this is my neighbor Shelley Nowack."

"I'm Maisie Valkenberg. I'm the set nurse for this misbegotten production. Neighbor which way?"

Shelley pointed.

"Then you'll be the honey wagons. And wardrobe goes on the other side."

"Honey wagons?" Shelley asked.

"Dressing rooms for the principal actors. Rest rooms for the rest of the cast and crew. The truck coming between your houses a few minutes ago was one of them."

Jane poured Maisie a fresh cup of coffee and took it to the microwave to nuke it to the boiling point. When she came back, Maisie was nibbling a cookie and saying, "Have you ever watched a movie being made before?"

"Only when my parents took us on the obligatory trip to California when I was a child," Shelley said. "We toured a studio, but I don't remember it looking anything like this."

"No, the studios are sanitized. Especially the ones that allow tourists. Location work is a whole different game. You'll probably enjoy it a lot. It's a weird, inbred little world and probably very different from what you'd imagine. My base will be by craft services. Bring your lawn chairs out tomorrow when they start filming and I'll try to explain anything I can."

"Won't we be in the way?"

"Not if you stick with me. They're putting up a fake building to shield the 'innards' of the production from the camera's sight. We'll be able to peek through. Just don't invite everybody you know."

"What about the kids?" Jane asked. "My son's school is having an in-service day tomorrow. He's dying to watch."

"How old is he?"

"Eighteen."

Maisie nodded. "Let me see if I can't find him something to do. Some kind of gofer job. He'd have fun."

"That would be great! Tell us about the movie," Jane said, handing around the cookie plate again just above Willard's reach. "The people who contracted with us for our backyards didn't tell us anything. What's the story?"

"As it happens, I sort of know. I don't usually even see a script because I don't need to, but this one's based on a book I read and really liked a couple years ago. The working title is *The Chicago Fire*, but the marketing dweebs will rename it. Probably *Secret Flames* or something. We're moving fast. Only five days on this location, including setup. The rest of the film was done in studios and these scenes will wrap it up. If they're following the book, there should be two parts that happen here. The big scene with the refugees from the fire setting up a sort of camp and then another segment many years after the fire when the heroine comes back, having inherited the land where she was once a penniless, singed widow. It was really a great story. The first part, of course, involves mobs of extras—all doing their best to hurt themselves and come whining to me," she added with a martyred look.

"Who's going to be in it?" Shelley asked.

"Lynette Harwell is the lead."

"Lynette Harwell? I thought she was dead!" Jane exclaimed. "She won that Best Actress award for *Day of Love* and then dropped out of sight."

"Not entirely," Maisie said. "You just haven't been watching grade-B movies since then. She's starred in such memorable films as *Killer Women of the Andes*, *Horror Nite*, and something I swear was called *Wasted Efforts*, which was truly a wasted effort. There must have been another ten or twelve, but I'm glad to say I've forgotten the names. Real doggy films. But I don't believe she's made any movies for the last five years or so."

"Why? What happened to her?" Jane asked. "I saw *Day of Love* a half dozen times—I just rented it from the video store a month ago, in fact—and she was fantastic. Was that great performance just a fluke, or what?"

"No, she's good. She just made real poor choices because she was greedy. I think she figured she could overcome the roles, like Michael Caine does. Nobody holds it against him that he makes terrible movies. He still gets chances to make good ones, too. But karma must have been against Lynette. She probably did a couple dreadful movies and nobody gave her the opportunity to do another good one. Then, too, there's the bad luck thing—"

"Bad luck? What do you mean?" Shelley asked.

"Well, she's been on troubled sets where there were accidents, thefts, illnesses, financial problems. I was on one of those films. None of the bad things had anything to do with her, as far as I know, but people in this business are fanatically superstitious. If somebody gets the reputation for bringing bad luck to a set, it's damn hard for them to get work."

"Is that why she hasn't worked lately?"

"I don't know. I heard a rumor that she was carted off to a loony bin for some kind of intensive therapy. Probably drugs. But it might not be true at all. Maybe her manager just decided it was trendier to be in rehab than simply unemployed and put the rumor out himself."

"Then how did she get this job?" Jane asked.

"I have no idea. There's a lot of speculation about it. Most of it pretty rude. But this one may well be the role that revives her career. I've watched some of the dailies and she's doing a fantastic job. One day last week she did a scene that even had the grips wiping their eyes. It's astonishing."

Jane was reveling in the conversation. All this inside poop on the famous was like having "Entertainment Tonight" broadcast live from her living room.

But Shelley had the perplexed look of a woman who was trying to drag something out of deep storage at the furthermost recesses of her brain. "Wasn't she from around here?" she asked. "It seems to me that I knew somebody who knew somebody who knew . . . no, it was her brother. He used to live in the next suburb over. I think he was deaf and went to work for a school district down south."

"Why, yes. I know who you mean," Maisie exclaimed. "I remember her brother. He used to do her makeup, but got out of the business to teach the deaf. So they lived around here?"

"I'm pretty sure they did. I'm remembering an article in the Sunday supplement years ago when she won the Oscar. It said she was a 'home town girl' who started out here doing commercials and fashion shows."

"Shelley, you're right," Jane said. "Now that you mention it, I recall having a pretty heated discussion with someone about how I remembered seeing her doing the weather on one of the local stations once, but I was told I had rocks in my head. I'll bet I was right. It was—oh, sixteen or seventeen years ago that I saw her doing the weather. When Mike was a baby."

Maisie grinned. "Watch out with that 'years ago' talk. She still pretends she's barely thirty."

"No!" Jane exclaimed. "She's my age, at least."

"Come on, Jane. Nobody's that old," Shelley said, with a grin. "Who else is in this movie, Maisie?"

"The principal male is George Abington. Do you know him?"

"I don't think so," Shelley said.

"Sure you do, Shelley," Jane said. "He was in a spy series on television for a couple years, then he showed up on all the game shows for a few more years. Real good-looking, but seemed like an ordinary kind of guy. He was married to Lynette once, wasn't he?"

"Jane, you amaze me, the junk you know," Shelley said.

"They *were* married once. For about five minutes," Maisie said. "It was during the movie I worked on with her ages ago. She'd just married George in a big splash of publicity, then they both went off to do some potboiler that Roberto Cavagnari was directing. Before the film was even in the can, she'd filed for divorce and moved in with Cavagnari."

"Who's Cavagnari?" Shelley asked. "Should I have heard of him, too?"

"Probably not," Maisie answered. "He's done a ton of high-testosterone things. *Terminator*-type movies. Spaghetti westerns. War stories. I can't imagine why he was hired to do this movie, but like Lynette, he's doing a great job. Far better than you'd ever expect."

Jane forgot herself so much that she put her cookie down where Willard could get it. "You mean Lynette Harwell is starring opposite George Abington, the man she abandoned for Cavagnari, the same man who's directing this movie?"

Maisie smiled wickedly. "Stranger things have happened in this business."

"Stranger, maybe. But that sounds downright dangerous," Shelley said.

Maisie got up and started putting her layers of clothing back on. "As I said, you'll find watching the process very, very interesting."

—— 3 ——

Vehicles and people kept arriving until well after ten o'clock that night. Jane watched, fascinated, from the back windows of the living room. An enormous piece of equipment that she later learned was called a condor, unfolded itself and lifted bright lights attached to a cherry picker–type basket high above the activity. The huge floodlights illuminated the field with harsh, heavy shadows. It was a truly eerie atmosphere, reminiscent of the scenes she'd sometimes seen on the news of nighttime catastrophes. It wouldn't have been inconceivable to discover a downed airplane in the midst of the scurrying mob of technicians. All that was missing was the wail of sirens and the flash of red lights. The noise and mob and sense of purposeful urgency were all there.

From the moment they'd come home from school and seen the extent of the production, Katie and Todd, Jane's two youngest children, both had been enraged that Jane wouldn't let them go out and wander around in the midst of it. "Just in the backyard, Mom," Todd pleaded after a quick, early dinner. "I'll take Willard out to his pen."

They were all crowded around the window with the best view. "You know he's afraid to go in the pen with anybody but me," Jane said, looking at the dog with irritation. "The big sissy."

"Poor old Willard is going to be one constipated doggy by the end of the week, aren't you, boy?" Mike said, grabbing Willard's ears and wrestling his head around—to Willard's absolute delight.

"Mike, please don't talk about the dog's digestive tract," Jane said with a shudder. Mike had given the dog a banana a week earlier, with results Jane was afraid she was never going to be able to forget.

"Come on, Mom," Katie nagged, tossing her hair dramatically. Katie was at the age that nearly all her conversations with her mother involved hair-tossing, flouncing, and/or door-slamming. Often all three. Jane had to keep telling herself that someday Katie would be a nice young woman and a wonderful companion to her—if they both survived her teenage years. "We won't go any farther than our own yard."

"This week it isn't *our* yard. I've rented it to the movie company. Part of what they're paying for is us staying out of their way."

"Aw, Mom. Let them go," Mike said. "They've got a security guy to keep people out. He won't let them get in the way."

Instead of being grateful for his older brother's help, Todd turned on him furiously. "Stop being so . . . so . . . *big*!" Todd sputtered. Jane suspected he'd rejected a number of adjectives that were popular among sixth grade boys, but wouldn't have gone over well at home. "Just 'cause you don't have to go to school tomorrow and the next day! Mom! Please can't I please stay home, too?"

"Todd, you know you can't. But they'll still be working when you get home from school anyway. You'll get to see plenty."

"Mom, it's just not *Fair!*" Katie whined.

Jane gave her a look.

"Yeah, yeah," Katie said. She raised her hands like a conductor and the boys joined in the chorus of Jane's oft-repeated line, " 'Life isn't fair.' "

The argument sputtered on throughout the evening and became more wide-ranging. Jane was accused of being an insensitive mother, obsessive about meaningless academic considerations at the cost of her children's social and intellectual development. Not that Todd had the vocabulary to put it that way, but that was the point.

Katie tried a pity ploy, not having caught on yet that crying didn't dissolve her mother's hard heart, but merely drove her to a frenzy of irritation. Then Katie moved on to guilt, working up an imaginary scenario in which Jane, unreasonably favoring her firstborn, had somehow suborned the school district in advance to let the high school be off for the exact day filming was to start, therefore deliberately slighting her two youngest children, whom she probably never wanted to have anyway.

Jane found herself actually wondering what *had* made her think it was a good idea to have three children. But she held firm, not because she believed that missing school would have been such a bad thing, but because she knew they'd inch closer and closer to the production if they were allowed to stay home and eventually get in trouble for which she'd be held responsible.

It didn't help that Mike was really being insufferably smug and adult about the fact that he'd been promised some kind of job, however menial, on the set.

Jane finally escaped her bickering progeny by pleading mending that needed to be done so that she could go hide from them in the minuscule guest room where she kept the sewing machine. When she looked out that window around ten-thirty, the floodlights had been turned off, vans full of workers were just pulling away, and a security guard was standing in her backyard talking on a mobile phone.

She already felt exhausted from having the movie filmed in her backyard and the filming hadn't even started yet. She sighed, remembering that she'd meant to get Katie aside sometime this evening and break the news that she and Mel were going to New York for the weekend.

But she hadn't the energy left for another confrontation. And teenage girls, like dogs, could sense fear and use it to their advantage. No, this wasn't the time.

Mike was up at the crack of dawn and woke Jane to ask which jeans he ought to wear.

"Jeans?" Jane asked blearily, trying to get her eyes open far enough to discern some difference between the two pairs he was showing her. "It's still dark. What time is it?"

"Almost six," Mike said. "I think the ones with the pocket torn off, don't you? The ones with the hole in the knee don't look serious enough."

Jane sat up in bed, shielding her eyes against the vicious glare of the bedside lamp. "Mike, I'd put those in the trash. They're both awful. You have a new pair in your top drawer. Wear those."

He looked at her with surprise. "I can't do that, Mom. They're new."

"Yes. And outrageously expensive, I might add."

Mike knew she was still half-asleep and was dreadfully patient with her. "Mom, I'd look like a kindergartner on the first day of school in those. Too eager. Like a . . . a . . . kid."

Jane shook her head, trying to clear it. "Okay, okay. The one with the pocket gone. Take the cats with you—" she called out as he headed for the door.

Max, a gray-and-black tabby, and Meow, a yellow butterball, were not happy at being scooped up and removed from her bedroom. They felt it important to be on the scene when she got up in the morning, just in case she'd been sleeping with a can of cat food that she might open any second. The fact that this had never happened didn't deter them from believing that it might.

They muttered behind the closed door while Jane got dressed and they twined themselves around her ankles as she headed for the kitchen. She'd just plugged in the coffeemaker and started the can opener when there was a knock at the door. The cats howled protests at this interruption of her activities.

Maisie was at the door. "Good morning," she chirped.

"It's only six-fifteen! How can you say that?" Jane exclaimed.

"Oh, I've been here for a half hour already. Is your son ready? I have some things he can do. Send him along."

Jane bellowed up the stairs for Mike and got him on his way, then got the cats fed and a cup of coffee inside herself before rousting out the other two kids. As soon as she heard movement upstairs, she took Willard out to his new dog run. He cowered and groaned in protest at first, but when he discovered that someone had tossed a half-eaten donut into the run, he settled in as if it were a home away from home.

Todd accepted the inevitable and went off to school without much fight. Katie tried to claim a horrific case of cramps, cramps that might well go down in medical history, but decided she didn't feel *that* bad when Jane made clear that staying home from school would mean staying in her own bedroom, which faced the front of the house, all day. Jane went back outside to drag Willard back indoors while Katie was reluctantly getting ready for school.

When she had her car pools done, Jane returned to the house, put on a minimum of makeup, brown corduroy slacks, and a peach-colored sweatshirt before strolling into the backyard. Shelley was sitting on a lawn chair next to Maisie. They'd situated themselves next to a snack spread of epic proportions.

"Help yourself," Maisie offered as Jane goggled at the long plywood table and the coolers beneath it.

There were drinks of every description: milk, buttermilk, skim milk, orange juice, pineapple juice, apple juice, coffee, cocoa, a dozen kinds of tea in bags. There were donuts and fruit bars, little plastic bags of sunflower seeds and peanuts and candy bars. She counted six kinds of chips and four kinds of bread besides bagels, donuts, and sweet rolls. There were fresh fruits and vegetable crudités, cookies, cheeses, spreads, dips, and all the makings for every kind of sandwich imaginable.

"There's enough food here for a hundred starving people," Jane said in wonder. Her stomach growled.

"That's about what we've got today," Maisie said. "Dig in. You can't make a dent."

"Is this normal?" Shelley asked. "All this food?"

Maisie nodded. "It's one of the best things about the job. The food. You should have seen breakfast."

"You mean this *isn't* breakfast?" Jane asked, biting into a sweet roll.

"No, the caterers' truck just left. Breakfast was a hot meal for everybody a couple hours ago. I'd weigh three hundred pounds if I worked very often."

They chatted with Maisie about her job and discovered that she was a military wife and an actor's daughter. She had combined the two with her nursing degree and had worked on many movie sets over the years as she followed her husband's postings. "Fortunately he was assigned to desk work in L.A. several times back when nearly everything was done in the studio. I worked a lot then," she said. "And now that so much work is being done on location, the number of jobs elsewhere in the country is increasing."

"You mean you live here in Chicago?" Jane asked. "Is anybody else local?"

"Oh, yes. Quite a few. Transportation, extras casting, all the extras, catering, craft services," she said, rattling off individuals by their jobs instead of names. "All local. Even Jake there is local now."

"Who's Jake?"

Maisie popped a donut into her mouth to free a hand and pointed to a tall man in his early forties who was leaning against a piece of fake building, obscuring their view of the set. He had shoulder-length maroon-red hair. As they looked at him, he made some semaphore-like gestures to somebody with his arms, then turned toward them as if he'd sensed their gazes. He was very fair-skinned, with lean, distinctive features that would have made him seem more likely to be in front of the cameras than behind them. He wasn't handsome in a traditional sense, but he was striking-looking and sexy in a bizarre, hazardous way. He looked like the sort of man who, in another age, might have come over from Ireland and led labor revolts.

—and cheated on his wife, Jane thought as he approached them with a dazzling, wolfish grin.

—— 4 ——

In spite of her better judgment, Jane was flattered at the interested look on Jake's face—until she realized it wasn't meant for her.

"Baby, you're killing me with those sexy outfits!" he said with a laugh.

Jane turned around to find a young woman approaching from behind. She was in her twenties and extremely pretty, but dressed and made up as a turn of the century escapee from a fire. Her long chestnut hair was deliberately disordered and there were sooty smudges on her face and arms. She wore a baggy gray dress with what Jane assumed were artificial sweat stains and ragged tears in the skirt and sleeves. "You old flatterer!" this young woman said, blowing a kiss at Jake as she went by.

He watched her, then reluctantly turned back to Maisie, ignoring Jane and Shelley as if they were no more than inanimate objects. "You don't happen to have seen Bobby's fancy watch, have you?" he asked.

"By 'Bobby' I assume you mean Roberto? The director?" Maisie said coolly. It didn't take a rocket scientist to figure out that Maisie wasn't crazy about

Jake. "If he hears you call him that, your ass is grass."

"Oh, Bobby wouldn't mind. He and I are old chums. Seriously, he's lost his Rolex. He thinks he took it off when you bandaged up his finger this morning."

"If he did, he just put it in his pocket. I didn't pay any attention. I think he got some coffee after I was through with him. Maybe he set it down over there," Maisie said, gesturing to the loaded-down craft service table.

Jake wandered off, looking around the table and taking nibbles of half a dozen things.

"The director hurt himself?" Jane asked.

Maisie started laughing. "It was, honest-to-God, a hangnail. He's just a raving hypochondriac. Oh, dear . . ."

A pair of young women were approaching them, one head down, crying. The other had her arm around her and was muttering to her comfortingly. Maisie got up to meet them and as the sobbing young actress raised her head, Maisie said, "Oh, you poor dear. It's chicken pox, you know."

"I can't have chicken pox!" the girl wailed. "I'm not a kid and I've got my first line today! I've never gotten to say a single word in a single movie and I'm supposed to do a whole scene with Miss Harwell this afternoon!" She'd gotten so pale that the telltale spots stood out even brighter.

"I'm sorry, honey, but you're not going to get to say a word in this one either."

Her friend spoke up. "I talked to Carl in makeup. He said they can cover the spots."

"Maybe so, but that's not the point. Chicken pox is a disease. A highly infectious disease that can be very tough on adults like you who missed having it as kids. I can't let you stay and pass it on to the whole crew—if you haven't already. Thank God we'll be wrapped before the incubation period is over!"

A crowd had gathered around them by this time, clucking curiosity, sympathy, and surprise. But Jane noticed that Jake, standing at a little distance, looked pleased. He suddenly dropped the roll he was munching on into a trash barrel and abruptly plunged between the fake buildings onto the set itself.

A young man with earphones standing by the table suddenly raised a bullhorn to his lips. "Quiet on the set!" he bellowed.

The unexpected blast of sound nearly flung Jane and Shelley out of their chairs.

"Quiet on the set!" they heard echoed two or three times from various distances, then another bullhorn voice squawked, "Rolling!"

A complete and stunning silence fell over the entire production. It was so quiet, Jane realized, that if she'd closed her eyes, she wouldn't have believed another human being was anywhere near. And yet there were probably a hundred people milling around chatting only a second before.

The girl with the chicken pox was led away, her shoulders heaving with silent sobs, and Maisie came back to join them. Jane started to whisper a question, but Maisie hushed her with a finger to her lips.

Everyone stood frozen. Most of the snackers, under the fierce eye of the boy with the bullhorn, had even quit chewing. Finally, after what seemed like five minutes of suspended animation, the distant bullhorn bellowed, "Cut!" and everybody came back to life. Conversations were resumed mid-syllable, a held-back sneeze erupted, the sound of hammering was resurrected, and everyone was once again in motion.

Shelley was bright-eyed. "I should have let the kids stay home to see this! And then I could have gone out and bought my own bullhorn and they'd have taken me seriously!"

A mob of people in tattered, burned clothing suddenly came crowding through the little space between the fake buildings and headed for the food like a swarm of locusts. A few gathered around a coffee can with sand in the bottom that sat on the ground a few feet away. They, the smokers, avidly lighted up.

Jane watched and listened with fascination to an ethereal, pious-looking girl who was dressed as a nun and was saying, " . . . so I told him I wouldn't ball a baldheaded guy if all my girlfriends swore he was the biggest stud in the world."

Shelley and Jane both burst into laughter at the incongruity of it.

A plump, frazzled woman in her sixties pushed through them and approached Maisie. "Nurse! Nurse! That girl with the awful spots! What did she have?"

"Just chicken pox, Olive. Nothing to worry about.

I've sent her home. Miss Harwell has had chicken pox, hasn't she?"

The older woman sighed with relief. "Yes. When she was only four and a half, poor darling. She was terribly sick. Can you only get it once?"

"Yes, only once."

"Well, that's good. Thank you. I'll just take Miss Harwell some nice herb tea and tell her not to be concerned."

They waited until the woman was out of earshot, busily fussing around the craft service table, before Jane whispered to Maisie, "Who in the world is that?"

"That is Miss Olive Longabach, Lynette Harwell's lifelong keeper. Apparently she was some kind of governess or nanny when Harwell was a kid and just stayed on with her. She's listed on the tech list as Harwell's 'dresser,' but she's dresser, keeper, social secretary, and all-round mother tiger. Poor old thing has no life of her own at all."

"I need an Olive Longabach of my own," Jane mused. "Where do you think I might pick one up."

"Just get yourself born into wealth in your next life," Shelley said, then after a pause added, "or be born a man and get married."

Since filming had apparently been suspended for the moment, Jane got up and edged close to the nearest fake building. There was, as she had hoped, a bit of a setback to one of the flats and she was able to peer out between them and see a slice of the field.

She'd looked at this abandoned area, without

really seeing it, for nearly twenty years, but it was virtually unrecognizable now. It was literally crammed with people and equipment. Not merely actors and cameras—she would have expected those—but dozens of people in grubby modern dress, all appearing extremely busy, and enough lights and stands to illuminate a baseball stadium. There were twelve-foot-square screens on frames set here and there and the hulking condor with the floodlights was being moved, chugging along snaillike as young men slapped sheets of plywood in front of its treads so it wouldn't sink into the ground.

There was also, to Jane's delight, a straggling row of tall wood and canvas chairs with the principal actors' names stenciled on them. "Just like in the movies!" she whispered to herself, grinning.

The sheer clutter of it was amazing. It seemed as though everybody on the whole set had brought some kind of bag along, some of them very nearly suitcase-sized. These were piled in heaps, thrown in odd corners, slung over the uprights of the chairs, and all the miscellaneous objects in one area were being moved as she watched. The actors' chairs, with the books, bags, knitting, and snapshot cameras associated with them, were being hauled off to a new site. Bags, light stands, and big electrical cables were likewise being dragged away.

Suddenly, a voice only inches away, but on the opposite side of the building flat, startled her. "Such a very nice boy you are."

Jane recognized Lynette Harwell's distinctive tone. For some reason Harwell's voice always reminded Jane of the old-fashioned phrase "Ashes of Roses." Elegant, extremely feminine without being shrill, understated, a little husky. No, more whispery. *I'm standing a few inches from a movie star!* Jane thought.

"I wonder if you've ever considered going into the business? With that profile and physique, you could probably get tons of work. And beefcake never goes out of style, you know," Lynette was saying.

"Not really, ma'am. I just live nearby and thought this would be fun," Mike answered.

Mike. This woman was talking to her son Mike about going into the movies! Horrified, Jane almost burst through the scenery before she could get a grip on herself. The dirty old woman! Talking to Mike— *her* Mike—about beefcake! This was an obscenity! And to think how she herself had helped Mike get on the set. It was like a mother mouse shoving her young into a cage of eagles!

Apparently they moved away because, try as she might, Jane couldn't hear either voice again. She stood there fuming for a moment before someone else approached the other side of the scenery.

She heard footsteps rustle the grass, then an unidentifiable voice saying, "What is it? I've got things to do."

"It's about that scene this afternoon. The kid who was supposed to be in it has come down with something."

"Shit! Does Roberto know?"

"Yeah. But you know what I want and I need your help."

They were speaking in emphatic whispers, a gravelly, unisex sound. Jane had no idea who was speaking or even what sex they were.

"I'm not on good terms with Roberto. It's all we can do to stay in the same state together without killing each other. I'm not gonna fight your battles."

"I wouldn't walk off if I were you, and I wouldn't take that attitude either," the first voice said, low with menace.

Jane was practically leaning against the flat.

"What's that supposed to mean?" the second unknown said. Even filtered through the scenery, there was just the smallest hint of fear in the voice.

"You don't want to forget that we go way back together. Remember *Bambi's Bed*? And *Frat House Orgy*? Wonderful films. A great credit to your acting skill."

There was a long pause, then the second voice said, "How do you know about those?"

"I know, that's all. Think what the media would make of it," the first went on. "You know, I don't believe they've ever given one of those presidential honors or Oscars or anything else to anybody with porno films on the old credit list. Maybe you'll be the first."

Whatever response the second speaker gave must have been with a gesture, because no more words were spoken. Jane heard somebody walk off and then the unknown voice muttered, "Son of a bitch!"

—— 5 ——

Jane staggered back to where Shelley and Maisie were talking and sat down heavily on her lawn chair.

"What's wrong?" Shelley asked. "You look like somebody's been slapping you around with a baseball bat."

Maisie wandered off to refill her coffee cup.

"A couple things," Jane said, trying to sound calm. "I've just been listening to a blackmail attempt not to mention somebody talking dirty to my own child."

"My, you *do* get around," Shelley said.

Jane explained first about the conversation she'd overheard between Mike and Lynette Harwell.

Shelley listened with a tolerant expression. "Jane, you're exaggerating this in your own mind. She was probably just trying to be helpful. In a tacky way, I'll admit," she said.

"Shelley, you didn't hear her. It was downright Mae West–ish! Seductive! You know that voice she's got; she could soften up an eggshell just by talking to it."

"Jane, I don't mean to depress you more, but Mike's a few months away from going to college.

32

You've got to trust that you raised him right, and you know you have."

Jane considered. "No, I think I'll just take him home and lock him in his room until he's thirty. There are good educational channels on television. He can learn from them. It's all because I agreed to go away for the weekend with Mel. I've set a depraved example and ruined him."

Shelley laughed. "Mike isn't ruined. It's Harwell who's got a problem. She's old enough to be his mother!"

"Oh, God! Don't say *that*!" Jane groaned.

But Shelley was on a roll. "Besides, if somebody were to seduce him, better her than some bimbo teenager who might end up as your pregnant daughter-in-law."

"Shelley, have you ever thought about going into the business of professional counseling?"

"No . . ."

"Then don't. You wouldn't be good at it."

Shelley smiled. "Jane, you do know you're going off the deep end, don't you?"

"Yes, but I thought a nice plunge into despair might be an antidote to the cheerfulness I've been feeling lately. I don't feel I'm being a good mother if I don't worry myself into a froth about something fairly regularly."

"So what were you saying about blackmail?"

"Blackmail? Oh, yes! While I was standing over there I heard somebody trying to persuade somebody to talk to the director about doing something."

"Oh, that is enlightening!" Shelley said. "Who are these somebodies?"

"I couldn't tell. But it was real blackmail."

"Is this the same kind of berserk overstatement you were making about Mike and Harwell?"

"No, not at all. The one person was saying he or she had some kind of proof about the other person being in porn movies and how they never give prestigious awards to people like that. And this person would keep it a secret if the other one would talk to the director."

"But about what?"

"I don't know. But they both seemed to."

"Surely you have some idea of whether it was a man and a woman or two men or whatever?" Shelley asked.

"No, not really. I have the impression it was men, but I know it's only because it was a brutal kind of conversation I don't associate with women . . ."

"You ought to get to a beauty shop more often to be cured of that idea," Shelley said.

"What are you two plotting?" Maisie said. Jane and Shelley hadn't noticed that she'd rejoined them.

In an undertone, Jane repeated to Maisie what she'd overheard.

Maisie shook her head in disgust. "The blackmailer was probably Jake. He's that sort of unprincipled person. It's a wonder he's still walking and breathing. As far as I can tell, he's mortally offended nearly everyone he's ever worked with."

"Then how does he get work? Doesn't the director know him? Why would he hire him?" Jane asked.

"Oh, Jane," Maisie said. "The director doesn't hire him. The director is just an employee like everybody else, although he's a very important employee and would never admit to being part of the 'hired help.' It's the producer who puts the whole staff together. And the reason Jake gets work is because he's so fantastically good at what he does. He just sits here in the middle of his vast national spiderweb of contacts and can lay his hands on any object you'd ever imagine. You want an eighteenth century tea service or a Revolutionary era spinning wheel or a Meissen toilet—you name it and Jake produces it without any fuss or bother. It just miraculously appears. Nobody likes him much, but he's very, very good at what he does. It's the same way with the principal actors. An extra has to be very agreeable, but a principal—if they're good enough—can get away with murder."

Jane had been listening, but her mind had fastened on a detail. "Are there such things as Meissen toilets?"

Before Maisie could reply, Shelley asked, "So who's the producer on this production? Anybody we've ever heard of?"

"I'm not sure. It's a weird thing," Maisie said. "It seems to be a consortium of people, but the front man is a little nerd nobody's ever heard of. He hangs around twitching and gulping nervously and makes lots of phone calls checking in with whoever he represents. That's him over there on the phone now."

Maisie pointed to a rattled rabbit of a man speaking into the set telephone with his hand over the receiver so he wouldn't be overheard. "Sometimes the money people like to stay in the background and run things from there," Maisie went on. "Not often, but it happens."

"But you told the person in your office that you were going to be talking to the producer soon," Jane said, then regretted this proof that she'd been eavesdropping.

Maisie didn't seem to mind. "I lied," she said cheerfully. "But it got me what I wanted in a hurry."

"I've always wondered what a producer does. You always see that on credits," Jane said.

"Oh, the producer's everything," Maisie replied. "The producer acquires the property—the story, that is—hires everybody from the scriptwriter to the janitor, and, most important, rounds up the money to make the film in the first place. That's a huge undertaking. It costs millions and millions to make a film. Even a television movie costs three or four million these days."

Jane was only half listening. Her eyes had strayed from the producer's representative to Jake, who had reappeared and was having an intense whispered conversation with the young woman Jane had noticed him speaking to earlier—the pretty girl in the sweat-stained, scorched dress. He was looking pleased and smug, but this time the girl was obviously mad as hell. She had her hands on her hips and her pretty face was drawn into an unattractive scowl. She snapped something at him and tried to walk away, but he grabbed her elbow roughly and pulled her back. She looked down at his hand with an indignant expression, and he reluctantly turned loose of her. But now he was angry, too. His fair face flushed and his handsome features were pinched.

Jane nudged Shelley and pointed discreetly. Shelley, in turn, whispered to Maisie, "Speaking of the devil."

"Our little Angela doesn't seem exactly happy to have him leering over her," Maisie said in an undertone. "I'm glad. She seems like a nice girl. I wonder how she got herself tied up with him."

"Is she?" Jane asked. "Tied up with him, I mean."

"Good point," Maisie said. "Maybe not. He pays a lot of attention to her and acts possessive. But now that you mention it, I don't recall seeing any signs of his interest being reciprocated."

"Who is she, this Angela?" Jane asked.

"Just an extra," Maisie answered.

Their conversation was cut short by the entrance of the director into the craft service area—and "entrance" it was. Roberto Cavagnari was a stocky little tractor of a man with dark, flashing eyes, designer jeans, and a flamboyant green velvet poncho that would have looked effeminate on anybody less aggressively male. He didn't walk; he strutted. He didn't speak; he proclaimed. Underlings schooled around him like minnows around a handsome, glittering trout.

"Call the weatherman," he ordered in what sounded to Jane suspiciously like a fake Italian accent. "I won't have overcast sky today." Jane wondered if he really supposed that weathermen ordered the weather rather than merely reporting it. A toady ran to do his bidding.

"Mister Cavagnari, if I could just have a word wi—" somebody said.

But the underling's request was lost in the next declaration. "I will have coffee. Mocha. Extra sugar," Cavagnari announced. Another assistant rushed to do the maestro's bidding, but he stopped her with an authoritative snap of his stubby, beringed fingers. "No, I will prepare it myself so it's done correctly," he said in the tones an empress might have used to say she'd do her own mending. Underlings fell back, nearly bowing, as he approached the snack table.

"*Ja, mein herr*," Shelley said under her breath.

"I think you've got the wrong country," Jane whispered. "I think we're supposed to be chanting, 'Duce! Duce!' "

Shelley laughed and Cavagnari whirled and glared at them for a moment before turning back to the preparation of his mocha coffee.

A second later he bellowed, "Jake! Jake! Here she is, my watch! I told you to look here."

Jake materialized at his side. "I did look for it here. Not half an hour ago."

"You did not use your eyes, Jake. It was here, beneath a chip wrapper."

"I am very good at seeing objects! I searched thoroughly," Jake said firmly. "It was *not* here."

"But you see? Here . . . just here before my eyes." He slipped the watch on.

"I tell you it was not—"

"Enough, Jake! I have spoken. It is done."

Jake subsided, obviously furious at having both

his judgment and his eye for details questioned, but apparently unwilling to anger Cavagnari further. His eyes narrowed and he looked around the group as if daring anyone else to criticize him. Then his expression turned deeply thoughtful.

Cavagnari discoursed briefly on the proper way to prepare his coffee, most of his audience pretending rapt attention. Then, when it was done to his satisfaction, he sipped and said, kissing his fingertips and offering them to heaven, "Perfect! Now, we will do the close-ups of scene fourteen, then luncheon."

He swept away, underlings trailing like the train of a coronation gown.

"Wow!" Shelley breathed. "That's an extraordinary display of ego run amok."

Maisie nodded. "Yes, but would *you* cross him? Or insist on your own interpretation of a role? You've got to be pretty ostentatious to intimidate actors."

"Jake stood up to him pretty well," Janc said.

"Jake's a fool," Maisie said dismissively.

But Jane was still looking at Jake and was thoroughly chilled by the sight of the small, secretive smile on his face.

Shelley followed Jane's preoccupied gaze and said quietly, "He's scary, isn't he?"

"I don't know whether to be scared *of* him or *for* him," Jane said, involuntarily shivering.

6

The rest of the morning passed uneventfully, at least for the moviemakers. For Jane, every new discovery was an event. She started out by prowling carefully through her neighbors' yards. In her own was the craft service setup and the "location office," which consisted of a table covered with stacks of paperwork and a phone. Two "honey wagons," which was what the trailer-type dressing rooms with bathrooms were somewhat obscenely called, were parked on Shelley's property. These were divided into tiny cubicles with doors along the long side, on which were written the principal actors' names. Jane was dying to get a glimpse of the inside of a cubicle, but nobody was around them just then and she couldn't peep through any open doors.

The house to the other side of Jane's had the wardrobe changing tent and the meal tent. Both were crude arrangements. The meal tent just had long trestle tables and wooden folding chairs. There was an odd piece of equipment at one end that she discovered was a kerosene heater, used at breakfast when it was still cold outside. The changing tent had a men's entrance at one end, a women's at the other, and a sheet hung between. There were lightweight wardrobe racks standing around the perimeter and everybody changed in the center of each section.

The wardrobe truck itself was in the yard beyond. This contained more substantial racks and a desklike arrangement where a young man was intent on updating the apparently meticulous records kept on each article of clothing. There was a minuscule washer and dryer in the truck as well as a sewing machine and a setup for ironing. Jane had once been "backstage" at a circus and this looked much the same: all the necessities of life made miniature and portable at a moment's notice.

Jane wandered into the next yard where another young man was sitting smoking and knocking back a soft drink on the metal steps leading up into the back of another truck. "Hi! Can I help you?" the young man said in a friendly manner.

"No, thanks. I'm a neighbor, just looking things over. What is this truck?"

"This is props. I'm Butch Kowalski, Jake Elder's assistant."

"Glad to meet you, Butch. I'm Jane Jeffry. Are you and Jake responsible for those fake buildings? They're really impressive."

"Naw, that's the set decorator's job. Props are in charge of any objects that are used or touched. Set decoration's everything that's just seen."

Except for Maisie, this young man was the first person on the crew who was genuinely friendly and forthcoming. He looked like a thug, with muscles that started just below his ears. He had practically no neck at all and his biceps strained the sleeves of his plaid shirt. He had teeth that would have made an orthodontist rub his hands in anticipation of the challenge and he had an unfortunate New Jersey accent. But for all that, his smile was engaging and his eyes sparkled with good spirits.

"You don't sound like a Chicago native, Butch. Do you live here now?"

"Yeah, for as long as I'm with Jake. I still got a lot to learn."

"So you want to do this yourself? Be a prop man?"

"Property master, ma'am. Yeah. But I won't be ready for a while yet."

"So, what is all this stuff?" Jane asked, gesturing toward the interior of the truck. As she did so, she noticed a movement inside and a glimpse of orange fur. "Meow! What are *you* doing in there!" she exclaimed.

"Oh, is this your cat, ma'am?"

"I'm afraid so. I'm sorry—"

"Oh, it's okay. She's a nice little thing."

Meow, who normally ran for cover when a stranger was within a block, picked her way daintily through the truck and came up to Butch to have her chin chucked.

"You must have a real gift with animals, Butch. Meow doesn't like anybody but me, and she only likes me when she's hungry. You haven't seen the other one, have you. The gray tabby?"

"The one with 'Max' on his tag? Yeah, he's takin' a nap in the cab of the truck."

Jane sighed. "I'll take them home. It didn't

occur to me that I needed to shut them indoors this morning."

"Naw, don't do that, ma'am. They're having a good time and I like the company. I'll make sure they're back to you before we shut down for the night so they don't get shut in somewhere. Which house do you live in?"

Jane pointed it out, got Butch's repeated assurances that he'd be happy to keep tabs on her adventuresome cats, and went back to her own yard. Shelley had gone somewhere and Maisie was busy putting salve on an extra's insect bite. Jane wandered over to the table where the phone was. The table had colorful stacks of papers, each stack held in place against the breeze by an unopened soft drink can or other heavy object.

Most of the photocopied piles meant nothing to Jane: call sheet, second unit requirements, a chart that appeared to show which scenes would be shot which days. But one stack said clearly, "Welcome Packet." Jane looked around for somebody to give her permission to study this, and since no one radiated authority or showed the slightest interest in what she was doing, she helped herself to one packet and went back to her lawn chair to skim through it.

"Is it okay for me to look at this?" she said when Maisie was through with the extra.

"Sure. It's for anybody who's involved in the production and you're involved—in a way."

"Maisie, I was counting the people on the crew list. There are over a hundred of them and it doesn't

include a single actor! That's amazing. I had no idea
it took so many people to make a movie. But isn't
it awfully wasteful? When I was roaming around
earlier, there were a lot of people just sitting and
doing nothing."

"Like me right now? Well, it's a hurry-up-and-
wait kind of business. Everybody's an expert in
their special, narrow area and when they are needed,
they're needed desperately. But the ones who are
sitting and doing nothing at any given moment are
on instant call. We all have to be poised to do 'our
things' at a second's notice."

"Sort of like a mother," Jane said.

Just then a young woman in jeans and a denim
jacket approached with a clipboard. "Are you Mrs.
Jeffry from this house?" she asked briskly.

"Yes."

"I just wanted to let you know that we'll be
breaking for lunch in ten minutes and you can let
your dog out for an hour if you'd like." With that,
she made a check mark on her clipboard and moved
on up the block.

Maisie grinned. "As I said, there are a lot of very
specialized jobs."

Jane went indoors to get Willard, whose fear of
the dog run had come back full force. She had to
put his leash on him and lure him with a piece of
lunch meat to get him out the back door and then
he stopped dead in horror at the sight of all the
people in his yard. She hauled him to the pen and
left him cravenly glued to the inside of the gate to
the run while she went next door to put Shelley's
yappy little poodle into its run. By the time she'd

dealt with all the livestock, she returned to her own yard to find another table being set up.

"No, no. Not in the shade," Lynette Harwell was saying to three young men who were trying to get the table placed to her satisfaction.

Jane was fascinated by the sight of the movie star. Though Jane knew Harwell to be her own age, she looked like a slip of a girl in her old-fashioned costume and blond hair done in an artfully disarranged braided coronet. Even the slight smudges of makeup soot on her face were placed so as to emphasize her enormous blue eyes and high cheekbones. She looked absolutely stunning and not quite real.

Jane had always imagined that unearthly beauty of some stars was a camera illusion and that in the flesh, they would look like normal people, but this was obviously wrong. Lynette Harwell was awesomely beautiful. Jane edged closer to the group surrounding her, a group including an adoring Mike Jeffry, and she was pleased to see that there were faint lines of age in the star's gorgeous face—tiny lines radiating at the corners of her eyes, a hint of the softness that precedes crepeyness on her throat, and the merest suggestion of the onset of a sagging chin. But these signs of aging only added character to the astounding beauty rather than detracting from it. Still, when you got close to her, it was clear that she was forty, not twenty—as her role demanded she look.

And as Jane gawked at her, Lynette turned to Mike and whispered something to him with an intimate smile that chilled Jane to the core, especially when she saw Mike's reaction. He grinned, looked at his feet, and all but scuffed his toe in the grass in pleased embarrassment.

She's playing mind games with MY child, Jane thought furiously. That her "child" was eighteen and had always been remarkably self-sufficient made no difference. She'd have felt the same if he'd been a fifty-year-old "Captain of Industry."

"Yes, just there is perfect," Lynette was saying, sweeping forward to take her place at the table. Like Queen Victoria, she didn't look back to see if a chair was in place, she just sat down, confident that someone had taken care of it. Which they had.

"I'll get your lunch," Mike said. "What would you like? The menu on the catering truck said prime rib or grilled shrimp."

"No, no! I will get Miss Harwell's luncheon tray!" Olive Longabach said. She'd just caught up with them and was breathless and disconcerted by having lost sight of her charge, however briefly. "I know what she likes."

"Olive, dear, there's no need. Mike can do it," Lynette said, positively *twinkling* at Mike. But Olive looked as if she'd been stabbed in the heart and Lynette relented. "Oh, very well, Olive. Mike will stay here with me, won't you, dear?" She gestured for him to sit beside her.

Jane snatched up her lawn chair and plunked it and herself down at the table before anyone could stop her. "How do you do, Miss Harwell. I'm Jane Jeffry. Mike's mother."

Lynette glanced at Jane for a fraction of a second, but didn't acknowledge her except with a slight compression of her lips. It was an unfortunate expression.

It showed up the "drawstring" wrinkles just starting around her mouth. Then she turned away. "Roberto, darling! Sit here with me! And George! Here!"

It was said in that soft, sexy voice, but it was an order just the same.

"May I join you, too?" Jake had approached just behind the director and the male lead. He was "technical" rather than "talent" but was apparently highly enough placed to horn in without violating the rules.

"Of course, Jake." A monarch granting a favor.

"Why don't you go get your lunch, Mom?" Mike asked in a tone that verged on hostility.

Sensing that her place would disappear if she did, Jane said, "Thanks, Mike. But I'm not hungry. I'll just sit here."

Mike stared at her as if to make her feel guilty for spoiling his lunch with Lynette. But, since that was exactly what she meant to do, Jane held her ground.

7

Jane listened carefully as they all chatted while luncheon trays were being delivered to them. She thought sure she'd recognize the voices of the blackmailer and the victim, but she could not. They were all speaking in their normal voices and the ominous discussion she'd heard earlier had been in abrasive whispers.

Going over it in her mind, Jane decided the victim must have been an actor or actress. Obviously somebody who made their living in front of a camera, not behind it. Lynette Harwell? Possibly. Or maybe George Abington. But if George or Lynette were holding any grudges against anyone at this table, they weren't evident at luncheon. The chat was general, professional: discussion of the weather as it related to filming, talk of the schedule. Very mundane stuff.

Jane studied George, suddenly recognizing him as the hero in a movie the children had loved when they were little. George was in his fifties, trying desperately to look thirty-five. He held himself rigidly upright, even seated, making Jane suspect he was wearing some kind of corset-type underpinnings. His hair was longish and unrealistically black and when a breeze lifted a lock of it off his ear, Jane could see the faint whitish line of a face-lift. His eyes, likewise, were too blue to be natural and the lashes looked tinted.

But for all the fraudulence of his appearance, he was still handsome. His manner, perhaps natural, or perhaps taken on for the duration of the filming, was Old-World, flowery and courteous, at least to Jane. He was the only one at the table who acknowledged her existence. "What a nuisance it must be for you, having your neighborhood invaded this way," he said.

"On the contrary. It's fascinating," Jane said. "I had no idea how hard—and early—all of you have to work. I couldn't even be myself, much less another character, so early in the morning."

"Ah, but you're seeing only a part of it," George answered, looking critically at a tray of food that a gofer had put in front of him. He turned over a lettuce leaf as if expecting something slimy to be on the other side of it. "Between jobs we lie about eating bonbons—or having wild affairs, if you were to believe the media."

"That may be how you spend your time, George," Lynette drawled. "I for one live a very spartan, healthy life. Rising early, exercising—"

"As well I know," George said with an excessively capped smile. "I remember all the exercise you used to get lifting glasses of wine to your lips. So good for the muscles of the arm, I always thought."

Lynette glared at him for a second, then laughed with hollow merriment. "Darling, you know I don't drink. You must have been reading the sleazier tabloids. I don't know why that doesn't surprise me."

"At least I *can* read, my dear," he said, and winked at Jane, drawing her into the joke on his side. Jane tried to look pleasantly noncommittal.

Roberto Cavagnari joined them at this point with a tray piled high with food. "Jake, the campfires, they are not right. These people, they would be burning bits of buildings, not twigs and branches and natural rubbish."

Jake set down his fork and said, "I don't agree. Remember, they have fled the fire into the country. There would be no buildings and they certainly wouldn't have carried pieces of buildings with them as they fled."

Cavagnari apparently recognized the sense of this, but didn't want to back down, so he pretended he hadn't heard Jake and launched into a story of a film he had directed in Europe where a special effect fire had gone wrong and endangered the surroundings. The story was not only boring and pointless, but delivered with such drama and so extreme an accent that Jane couldn't follow it at all. Instead, she just studied the others, wondering which of them she had overheard earlier.

Lynette was picking daintily at her food, but managing to subtly put quite a bit of it away without looking piggy. She was gazing at (or through) Jake as she ate. She might well have been in a naughty movie in her youth, but her voice was so very distinctive that Jane couldn't have failed to recognize it if Lynette had been one of the unseen speakers. Jane certainly knew it was Lynette moments later when she overheard her talking to Mike.

Olive the Keeper stood behind Lynette, a sentinel. Her eyes were never still. Jane had once attended, unwillingly to be sure, a political rally where the vice president of the United States was present and had been fascinated by the way the Secret Service agents continuously examined the crowd the same way Olive Longabach was. It was as if she had it on reliable authority that a sniper was present.

And there were plenty, but the "snipes" were verbal and seemed to be bouncing off Lynette. Yes, Olive was the only one who appeared disconcerted, but it looked like an habitual attitude. And the idea of lumpy, frumpy Olive ever being in a skin flick was ludicrous.

Jane gave up speculating. After all, there were a hundred people on this set and there was no reason to suppose the two she had overheard were among those at this table. They were probably off someplace else right now, hissing more threats and excuses at each other.

Pretty, chestnut-haired Angela had unobtrusively taken a seat at the far end of the table and was keeping a low profile. Apparently she and Jake had sorted out whatever they'd been arguing about earlier in the day, or had at least decided to ignore each other.

Jake Elder had wolfed down his lunch and appeared to be listening to Cavagnari drone on. He looked quite interested and calm, except for his right hand. Jane guessed he was an ex-smoker, having a hard time passing up the after-meal ciga-rette, because his hand kept fidgeting wildly, as if it had a life of its own. It reminded her of *Dr. Strangelove.*

Mike, well-mannered as he was, was looking at Cavagnari intently, pretending great interest. But Jane knew the look on her son's face. She'd seen it often enough. Fake fascination, and behind it he was thinking about baseball or girls or how to talk her out of the use of the station wagon for the weekend. She was enormously relieved.

" . . . and by the time the fire trucks, they arrived, the fire was out!" Cavagnari finished up his story with a flourish. Jane and the rest took this to be meant as a humorous ending and she joined the polite tittering. The only one who made no pretense was Olive, whose face was set in a grim, angry mask, although what there had been in the story to offend her, Jane couldn't guess.

"This is great! Just great!" the producers' nerd said. "I've been taping you!"

"What!" Cavagnari and Jake objected in unison.

Only George Abington went on eating, bending forward at the neck slightly and confirming Jane's guess that his underwear prevented him from bending at the waist.

The young man came forward from where he'd been lurking. He had a camcorder. "Well, we'll need all the promotional clips we can get and I told "Entertainment Tonight" that I'd get some casual shots before their crew gets here. That was a great story, sir, and people will love seeing you tell it."

"I did not authorize this taping!" Cavagnari shouted. "I will not have it on my set!"

"But, Roberto, people like seeing the cast out of character," Lynette said softly. "I think it's a good idea."

Jane looked at the beautiful star and guessed that she alone had noticed the faint whir of the camcorder and had been eating so daintily because she realized that it was being filmed.

"No, no! I authorize filming!" Cavagnari shouted. "Nobody else!"

"I'm sorry, sir," the young man said. "But that's not quite right. The producers authorize—"

Cavagnari stood up, green poncho swirling, flung his chair aside, and lunged for the camera, wrenching it from the startled young man's grasp. Cavagnari pushed a button and popped the tape out. "The producers? The secret, chickenshit, afraid-to-show-their-faces producers? This is what I think of your producers!"

His accent had been pure Bronx for a moment. He strode to the trash container by the craft service table and dropped the tape into it with a flourish.

Then he thought better of that. Accent back on track, he said, "Ah-hah! I see your look! You think when my back is turned, you will come back and remove it!" He fished the tape back out and looked around for a means by which to destroy it on the spot.

"I'll throw it away if you like," Jane said.

"Who are you!" Cavagnari demanded.

"This is my yard. I live in this house," Jane replied sweetly. "I'll put it in the trash inside." *Maybe*, she thought to herself. Or maybe she'd just keep it as a nice little souvenir of having had lunch with a bunch of famous people. She noticed that Mike was smiling at her, making her wonder if her son could read her mind as well as she read his.

Cavagnari lobbed the tape at her, which she managed to catch before it hit her. Jane felt her face reddening with anger and embarrassment. This man needed to go back to preschool and learn manners from the ground up. She slipped the tape into the kangaroo pouch on the front of her sweatshirt.

The producers' representative was muttering fiercely to himself and studying his recently assaulted camcorder for damage.

"If I see you use that again, I'll smash it to bits," Cavagnari said to him.

A tense silence fell over the group. Only Lynette Harwell seemed immune. She was still eating; slowly, delicately, relentlessly finishing everything on her plate. Perhaps this was why Olive Longabach insisted on serving her, Jane speculated. Knowing Lynette's appetite *and* her need to stay slim, Olive probably chose precisely the number of calories Lynette could afford to eat.

Jane was still seething with anger at Cavagnari's rudeness, but she had come out of the scene with the tape and was feeling an odd hostessy urge to make conversation. After all, they were all eating in her backyard, even if she hadn't invited them. "I understand you're originally from Chicago, Miss Harwell," she said.

"Oh, hundreds and hundreds of years ago," Lynette said with a coy laugh, which was presumably meant to cue somebody to say that it couldn't have been so long ago.

Nobody did.

"From this part of town?" Mike asked.

Cavagnari fell to eating his lunch, having ignored it while telling his endless story. Jake was studying a script with notes in the margins. George was making conversation with two people at the far end of the table who Jane hadn't even noticed were there until now.

"No, we lived much closer in," Lynette said. "I was in my last year of high school and didn't know a soul. It was very lonely for me." This with an attractive little *moué* of sadness. "But I kept myself very busy. I did some modeling and community theater. And I studied privately with a very great old actress who had retired to the area and took only a select few students who she knew had great potential. Isn't that right, Olive?"

Olive, still on guard behind Lynette, merely nodded.

Lynette smiled at Olive. "Poor darling Olive would find me up fearfully late at night, going over and over my lines. Making sure I had it perfectly right. And she'd have to absolutely force me to sleep."

Olive finally softened. "You always did work too hard."

"But it was worth it, wasn't it, darling Olive."

To whom? Jane wondered. To Lynette surely, but to Olive? All that Olive had gotten out of it was a hard life on film sets and locations. Sleeping in strange hotels, having no life of her own, waiting hand and foot on a spoiled, aging seductress?

"Mom," Mike said suddenly. "I wonder if maybe I ought to take a few acting lessons. Just to see if—"

"Oh, my dear! You must! You might be terribly, terribly talented," Lynette gushed, putting her hand over his. "You certainly have the looks for screen work. In fact, you remind me of a great love of my life! I met him just before I left Chicago. He was such a handsome man and I adored him, but he was married. Such a tragedy! I always thought he should have thrown away his dreary little wife and his dreary little job and joined the great pageant of the acting profession. I was always saying to him, 'Steve, you're wasted here—' "

"Steve?" Mike repeated.

Jane's heart was in her throat as she leaped up. "I think somebody's calling you to the set, Miss Harwell."

"Steve who?" Mike asked, his voice husky. "The only person I look like is my dad."

Jane was already around the table, pulling on Mike's arm. "Honey, I need your help inside with some—"

"Steve Jeffry was his name. My, he was a good-looking man, and so romantic," Lynette went on, oblivious to Jane's attempts to shut her up.

Mike had stood, but he shook off Jane's hand and looked down at Lynette. "Are you saying you had an . . . an *affair* with Steve Jeffry?"

Lynette looked up, finally realizing something was wrong. "Yes. Why do you ask?"

Mike looked at Jane and said very quietly, "Because he was my father."

He turned and strode toward the house, pausing only to give a vicious kick to the barbecue grill.

"Oh, dear . . . perhaps I shouldn't have said . . ." Lynette was saying as Jane ran after Mike.

——8——

Mike was already in his room, slamming things around when Jane caught up with him. At her knock, he came out and barged past her, red-eyed and white-faced with anger.

"You knew!" he shouted, galloping down the stairs.

"No, Mike. I didn't know."

He stopped at the bottom and looked back up at her. "Yes, you did! You were trying to stop her. You knew what was coming!"

"I didn't *know*. I *suspected*. But not until it was too late."

"You knew! And you let me make an ass of myself, following her around, doing her errands, thinking she was—"

"Mike! What are you saying? I wouldn't do a thing like that to you."

"I'm going out!"

"Mike, I'm sorry . . ."

But she was talking to herself. The front door had slammed so hard she feared for the hinges.

She went to her bedroom and sat down on the bed. Of course Mike was furious at his father's betrayal. She'd felt the same way when she discovered that Steve Jeffry had been a philanderer. She'd felt anger, grief, humiliation, and a lot of other ugly emotions that didn't even have names. And she'd worked hard at hiding it from the children, knowing they would be devastated. Since Steve wasn't around to take the brunt of Mike's anger, it had come down on her. It wasn't reasonable, but it was understandable.

Jane felt chilled through and vaguely "dirty." She was still shaking and trembling and decided maybe a hot shower might help her calm down. As she headed for the bathroom, the videotape, which she'd stuffed into the front of her sweatshirt, fell out and hit the floor. She looked down at it with distaste. She'd meant to keep it as a memento of a remarkable luncheon, but she knew she could never watch it without remembering what had followed the taping. She kicked it under the bed. She didn't even want to touch it now. When she felt better, she'd pull it back out and destroy it.

There was a furtive tap on the door of the bedroom an hour later. Jane had stood under the hot shower until the water had started to run cold and her skin looked like a sunburned raisin. Then she'd dried her hair and put on fresh jeans and a clean white blouse. At least she was cleaner, if not exactly calmer.

She opened the door.

Mike slouched in. "I'm sorry, Mom. I acted like an asshole."

"It's okay. You're entitled."

"No, I'm not. It must have been just as awful for you as it was for me. I just wasn't thinking."

Jane hugged him long and hard.

When he finally let go of her, he said, "What did you mean about suspecting that was what she was going to say?"

Jane sat down on the edge of the bed and patted the spot beside her. "Sit down, Mike. I didn't want any of you children to ever know this, but I think I've got to tell you now. That night when your father was killed in the car wreck—he wasn't going on a business trip like I told everybody. He was leaving me—leaving us. For another woman."

"Jesus, Mom! You knew that? And you never told us?"

"Why should I have? Look at how angry and hurt you are about it now. I never wanted you kids to feel as awful as I did. I didn't know until today that there had been others, although I'd figured that there probably had been."

"Oh, God! What a jerk! And I thought he was a neat guy! I mean, he was my *dad*!"

"He *was* a neat guy, Mike. In a great many ways. I just wanted you to remember all the good stuff and not know about the bad. What good does it do you, knowing? None. It's just a truth that you'll eventually get used to. Believe me, as horrible as you feel this minute, it will fade. You won't stay mad forever. I know you can't imagine that right now, but—"

"I dunno. You've stayed pretty mad yourself."

"Why do you say that?"

"Well, I mean—the mess you made of the kitchen—"

"Kitchen?" Jane shook her head. "I don't know what you're talking about."

Mike stared at her for a long moment. "You, uh—you didn't kick things around the kitchen after I left?"

Jane stood suddenly. "I didn't go back downstairs," she said very quietly. "What are you talking about?"

She ran down the steps with Mike close behind her. The kitchen was a wreck. Cabinet doors were flung open, drawers were pulled out and gaping. Silverware was strewn around the floor; several broken dishes were in shards. And somebody had upended the wastebasket, which had been in dire need of emptying, in the middle of the room and scattered the trash—gum wrappers, the contents of an ashtray, the husks of the corn on the cob from last night, discarded rice mix packages, everything was everywhere! Max or Meow had walked through some spilled flour and tracked it into the living room.

"You didn't do this?" Mike asked.

"Are you crazy? I'm the one who cleans the kitchen! Would I do this to it?"

Mike reached for the phone. "Mom, go stand outside in the driveway. I'm calling the police. Somebody's been in the house and might still be here someplace."

Jane started to tell him he must go outside and she would remain behind to do the calling, but recognized immediately that Mike needed to be in charge right now and was obviously more capable than she at the moment. It hadn't even crossed her mind that the maniac who did this might still be close by.

She waited for Mike in the driveway for what seemed like hours, but was only a minute or two, then the two of them went and sat together on the curb until two patrol cars arrived. Jane was first furious, then frightened, then furious again. It was going to take her forever to clean up the mess—and longer still to get over the sheer "violation" of it.

"There's a prowler in your house, ma'am?" the first officer to emerge from his car asked.

"We don't know," Mike answered.

Both officers went inside, hands on their holsters.

While Jane and Mike waited, a red MG came tearing down the street and lurched to a stop. Mel Van Dyne leaped out. "Jane! Mike! Are you all right? I heard the call at the station. What's going on?" His usual cool sophistication, while not missing, was distinctly frayed around the edges.

"Somebody wrecked my kitchen. Probably a good cook, furious at the outrages I perpetrate there." She laughed nervously. There was the beginning of a sob somewhere in the laugh. "Two officers are inside now."

"What about the rest of the house?" Mel asked, putting a hand on her arm as if to physically keep her from flying off.

"We didn't stick around to look," Mike replied.

"Good thinking, Mike. Not many people have the sense to think of that in a crisis."

One of the officers came out. "Charlie's double-checking, but it seems to be empty."

"So when did this happen?" Mel asked.

Jane took a deep breath. "Mike and I came in by the back door about an hour ago. I didn't lock the back door—"

"Jane, I've warned you—" Mel began. His hand tightened on her arm.

"I was upset! I forgot!" she was nearly shouting. She took a deep breath. "Sorry. Anyway, Mike went back out the front door and I went upstairs and took a long shower, then dried my hair. I couldn't have heard anything going on downstairs. Mike came back about five or ten minutes ago and discovered the kitchen had been ransacked."

The other officer came outside. "It's clean, Mel."

"Clean? Hardly clean," Jane said, then wished she hadn't spoken. She was sounding a tad hysterical.

"I'll carry on from here. Thanks," Mel told them. When they'd left, Mel escorted Jane and Mike back into the house through the kitchen door. "Jeez, what a mess!"

"It's mainly the wastebasket trash, I think," Jane said, getting the broom and dustpan from the closet.

"No, hold up on that," Mel said. "Is there anything missing?"

"Mel, how would I know? And what would anybody want to steal from a *kitchen*, for heaven's sake?"

"You don't keep valuables in here, do you?"

"Not unless you count the antique meat loaf in the fridge. I'm thinking about donating it to the Smithsonian."

"Very funny, Jane," Mel said sourly. "Who have you offended lately who'd want to vandalize your house?"

"Only my mother-in-law. And don't dare ask!"

"Mike, you didn't see anybody leaving the house when you came in, did you?"

"No, but I came in the front. If they went out the back, I wouldn't have seen them anyway."

"I guess I'm going to have to ask that mob in your backyard then," Mel said, sighing.

"Backyard! Willard! I forgot to bring him in!" Jane said.

"I'll go get him," Mike volunteered.

When the back door closed behind him, Mel put his hands on her shoulders. "What's really going on here, Janey?"

He'd taken to calling her Janey in private since she accepted his invitation for a weekend together in New York and from him, she liked it. She let herself lean into an embrace. "Oh, Mel. It's a mess and I can't start explaining right now because Mike will be back in a minute. But I've got a problem and I don't know if I ought to leave home this weekend. Actually, it's Mike's problem now and I have to see if he's worked it out before I can decide."

"Are you saying Mike may have made this mess?"

"Oh, no! Not at all. This has nothing to do with the kitchen."

"Okay, Janey. We'll talk about it whenever you want. In the meantime, please keep your doors locked all the time. With all those people roaming around back there, you've seen how easy it is for somebody to slip in here. I'll go out and talk to their security people in a minute and tell them to keep a special eye on your house."

There was a commotion at the back door and Willard came shooting in and headed for the basement door. Jane opened it and he hurtled down the steps to safety. Mike came in, followed by Maisie, who was holding onto Butch Kowalski's arm. She was keeping his hand in the air and had a towel wrapped around it.

"What's happened?" Jane asked. Butch looked as white as death.

"Jane, I'm sorry to barge in on you this—what on earth?" She looked around the kitchen.

"Long story," Jane said.

Maisie nodded. "Okay. Butch cut his hand and I need to wash off the blood and see if it's serious or not."

Jane grabbed the broom again and made a quick, brutal swipe through the center of the room to the sink. As Maisie eased away the towel and started carefully running warm water over Butch's hand, Jane got the clean rag bag off the back of the basement door and handed Maisie a wad of cloth.

Butch was wavering, looking as though he might faint any moment, and Mel went around to stand by to catch him if he did. Finally, Maisie said, "All right, Butch my boy. It's not half as bad as I was afraid. No real damage. Just a lot of blood.

I'm going to wrap this for a few minutes until the bleeding stops, then I think I can fix you up fine with a few butterfly bandages. I don't think you even need stitches."

"Thanks," Butch said weakly.

"Come sit down here," Mel said, leading him to the kitchen table.

"Thanks. Who are you?" Butch asked. He sounded woozy.

"Mel Van Dyne. Friend of Mrs. Jeffry. Now sit down."

Maisie left to get her first aid kit and Mike helped Jane get the rest of the trash back into the wastebasket and close up the drawers and cabinets. Mel sat at the table, keeping a close eye on Butch.

Maisie came back with her kit. "You don't have a cold pack of some kind, do you, Jane?"

"Yes, in the basement freezer. Mike, would you—"

Butch suddenly came alive. "God! I'm supposed to be helping Jake with something! Could somebody find him and tell him where I am?"

"Who's Jake?" Mel asked.

"He's the property master. I work for him and he's gonna be mad as hell that I'm missing without telling him why!" Butch sounded ready to cry.

"Jane, open that kit, would you?" Maisie asked.

"I'll find him for you," Mel said. "What's his name again?"

"Jake Elder. He'll be in the props truck, two houses up the street," Butch said.

With Jane's help, Maisie got Butch's bleeding stopped. He had a nasty gash on his palm, but Maisie disinfected and dried the area thoroughly and "sutured" it with a tidy line of butterfly bandages. "How did you do this?" she asked him.

"I'm not sure. Jake sent me ahead to get the firewood stuff together and I was hurrying. I started to run up the metal steps to the truck and my foot slipped. I reached out and grabbed something to catch myself and came away with this. There musta been something ragged on the handrail of the steps."

"I'm going to splint your wrist, just so you don't accidentally move your hand around and pull those bandages loose," Maisie said.

Maisie was just finishing this when Mel came back inside. "This Jake . . . he's got long hair? Dark red? Wearing a blue shirt?" he said briskly to Butch.

"Uh-huh. That's him."

Mel reached for Jane's phone, dialed, and, while waiting for an answer, said, "I'm sorry to tell you, he's dead."

There was a collective gasp from Maisie, Butch, and Jane.

"Murdered," Mel added.

"I go away to do my library volunteer stint for three hours and when I come back all hell has broken loose!" Shelley exclaimed.

"And you don't yet know the half of it," Jane said.

They were sitting at Jane's back window again, but this time the activity outside was different. The property truck, just barely visible from their perspective two doors up the street, had been roped off with yellow plastic ribbon and police cars mingled with the movie vehicles. But, remarkably, the movie set was still busy. A scene was being filmed at the farthest end of the area from the police business.

A uniformed police officer and a police secretary had taken over Jane's hastily tidied kitchen and were questioning people one by one on their movements for the afternoon. Shelley and Jane had eavesdropped for a while, but the questions and answers were exceedingly dull routine ones and Jane assumed Mel was questioning the "important" players, because the officer in the kitchen was working his way through the list of extras and the most minor of the technical workers, getting names, addresses, accounts of movements. As almost nobody had paid attention to the time, he must have been getting frustrated. But he kept patiently plodding through his list.

"I assume you told Mel about overhearing the blackmailing conversation," Shelley said. "What did he say about that?"

" 'Just the facts, ma'am.' You know how stuffy and efficient he gets when he's on duty. He wanted to know where I was standing, when it happened, how loud the voices were, whether I recognized who was speaking, that kind of thing. I think he was already mad at me before this happened."

"Why?"

"Because I threatened to back out on our week end away."

"After buying all that new underwear? Why? Did Thelma scare you?"

"No, it's got nothing to do with Thelma."

Jane explained about the lunch in her yard and Lynette Harwell's devastating bit of information about her affair with Jane's late husband. "Poor Mike just unraveled. He stormed out of the house, hurling accusations at me. When he got back, he'd calmed down some, but you could tell he was crushed. Then, before we could even thrash it out, he mentioned what happened to the kitchen."

Shelley held up her hands. "Kitchen? Hold it! What are you talking about? Has this unhinged you completely?"

"I just hadn't gotten to that part yet. Somebody came in while I was showering and trashed my kitchen."

"Probably trying to find your recipe for cheese bread to destroy it before you destroyed the world with it," Shelley said with a smile, which faded quickly. "You aren't serious, are you?"

" 'Fraid so. Drawers jerked out and rummaged through, cabinets partly emptied. A few broken dishes. There were trash and pots and pans all over the floor and counters and flour everyplace. I managed to just sweep everything into the guest bathroom and close the door on it before the police took over the kitchen. That's why Mel was here. Mike called the police and so we were sitting here with Mel when Butch came in with his hand gashed—"

Shelley's mouth dropped open. "Butch? Who in the world is Butch?"

"Jake's assistant. A really nice kid. About twenty, New Jersey accent, no neck. He'd cut his hand pretty badly and Maisie brought him in here to wash it off and fix him up. He got all panicked that Jake would be mad at him for leaving his job, so Mel volunteered to pass the message along to Jake for him. Mel was going to go out back anyway and ask people if anyone had seen somebody coming in my house. Anyhow, Mel found Jake's body in the props truck."

Shelley shivered. "God, that's awful! How was he killed?"

"I don't know. Mel didn't say."

"So, while I was frittering away my time at the library, you unearthed a nasty family secret," she said, ticking off her fingers, "had your house vandalized, invited in a guest with a bloody hand, and sent another visitor out to discover a dead body? Jane, sometimes you amaze me."

"But I had nothing to do with any of it, except that I live here. It's not as if I pried the information out of Harwell—God knows I didn't want to hear about her and Steve—or went out searching for somebody to wreck my kitchen!"

"Mel's not going to see it that way," Shelley warned. "Especially if you're backing out on the romantic weekend."

"I don't know that I am yet. I still haven't had a chance to talk to Mike. I just don't want him to feel that I'm abandoning him at a bad time in his life. For him, this must be like losing his father all over again. First Steve died, and now even Mike's memory of him has to be drastically revised. That's tough, especially when you're still so young. Shelley, I told him about Steve leaving us the night he died. I didn't want him to ever know, but I heard myself telling him and I was appalled."

"Jane, he's a tough kid. He'll survive it and I've always thought you should have told him. He was bound to find out sooner or later. Better that it came from you. Where are your kids anyway?"

"As soon as Katie and Todd got home from school, Mike took my side about them not going out in the yard. Of course, he's just afraid they'll somehow find out what he learned. He took Todd to a movie, after getting into a screaming match with Katie. She's in the back bedroom watching out the window—and no doubt plotting revenge on Mike and me both. I could have used her help cleaning up the kitchen. It was an unholy mess, but I didn't want to have one more thing to fight about. With anybody."

Both women fell silent for a while, watching the activities outside and thinking.

In the kitchen, the police officer questioned a hippy-dippy individual who was expounding on why she never wore a watch and couldn't possibly tell him what time anybody did anything because time was an artificial concept that had caused most of the misery in the world and ought to be outlawed so that the fascist pigs couldn't try to trip people up by asking about it. To his credit, the officer just went on to the next question without any comment.

"Oh, Jane—what a lot you have to sort out," Shelley said quietly.

Jane sighed. "Oh, I don't know. The police have to sort out Jake's murder, and Mike has to sort himself out. All I have to do is stand by and be available if needed. In both cases."

Shelley nodded. "But aren't you curious? About Jake?"

"Madly!" Jane said, relieved to be talking about the one aspect of the hectic afternoon that least involved her. "I'm still trying to figure out whether the blackmailer I overheard was Jake. I'm inclined to think so, but I know that's partly because Maisie suggested it was the kind of nasty thing he'd do, and partly because he's dead and it would be a good motive. But I really had no *good* reason to think so. It might not have even been a man speaking. Maybe a woman with a low voice."

"Like Lynette Harwell?" Shelley suggested.

"That crossed my mind," Jane admitted. "But I know that's because I want to think badly of her. I mean, I already do, but I'd like to pile on the sins, so to speak. I don't honestly believe it could have been her voice, however."

"Just who was at this lunch?"

"Jake, Lynette Harwell, that weirdo director, George Abington, Mike, and me. Angela and somebody else I didn't recognize were at the far end of the table, but they didn't have much of anything to say."

"How did everybody act toward each other?" Shelley asked.

"Absolutely bland for the most part. As if they'd never met or had a cross word. Well, except for George Abington and Lynette Harwell. They sniped at each other, but it had a quality of old stuff that neither of them really had their heart in. Cavagnari was unaware of anybody except as an audience to listen to a confusing story about a set that blew up or blew down or something. I think it was in Prague, which is very possibly the most boring place on earth to hear about."

"What about Jake? How did he act?"

"No particular way. He didn't say much. He pretended to politely listen to Cavagnari. Ate all his lunch as if he had nothing especially important on his mind."

"You didn't sense that he felt he was in danger?"

"No. Not at all. But then, I didn't know the man. I wouldn't have any idea what's normal behavior for him."

They watched as Mel crossed the backyard toward the house. He came into the living room a minute later with the police secretary in tow. "Mrs. Jeffry, would you please repeat for the record what you heard earlier today? The conversation you overheard?"

Very formal, aren't we? Jane thought, and responded in kind. "Of course, Detective Van Dyne. I'm sorry, but I don't remember the exact words, only the gist. Two people were speaking—"

"Are you sure of that?"

Jane thought for a minute. "I think so. At least the context of the conversation suggested that there were only two. The first one said something about one of the actresses getting sick and that the other one knew what he wanted done. There was something about talking to the director and the second one said he and the director didn't get along and he wouldn't help. Then the first one said something about remembering some porn flicks and how they didn't give prestigious awards to people who had been in them."

"And . . . ?" Mel prodded.

"And nothing. That was it."

"Nothing more specific than that?"

"The blackmailer mentioned the names of some movies, but I don't remember exactly what they were. One was Something Bambi or Bambi Something. The other one had something to do with college. Classroom Capers or something like that."

Mel thought for a moment and the secretary sat with her pencil poised like an automaton with her batteries turned off.

"You keep saying 'he,' " Mel said. "Were the speakers both men?"

"I'm not sure. I thought they were, but I couldn't be positive. They were whispering."

"And you could hear them?"

"Whispering loudly," Jane said, feeling foolish. It *was* his job to pick holes in her story, but he didn't have to be so good at it. She was sure he was picturing her in the undignified position of having her ear glued to the back of the set, which was true.

"Okay. What about the way they spoke. I mean the grammar. Were they both educated sounding? Could you discern any accent? Any speech impediment?"

Jane considered carefully. "No, there was nothing remarkable in any way. Normal language. No glaring errors. No lisp or anything like that."

He asked a few more questions about the time of day she heard them, the duration of the conversation, and her proximity to the speakers, then dismissed the secretary. He walked over and stared out the back window for a minute. "These are the oddest people. Look at them. Everybody looks busy, but you can't tell exactly what any of them are doing. And they just keep doing it. Murder doesn't seem to faze them. I like for people to be taken aback by death. At least for a little while."

Mel seldom spoke seriously about his job and Jane was surprised. She and Shelley waited for him to go on, but instead he turned back to them and smiled. "You got your kitchen cleaned up, didn't you?"

"Not really," Jane admitted. "I just shoved most of the mess out of sight. I'll sort it out later and get things back to their proper places. Anybody who tries to use the guest bathroom is in for a horrible shock."

"Anything missing?" Mel asked.

"Who could tell? I doubt it. Mel, you haven't told us . . . how was Jake killed?"

"Stabbed. And the knife was jammed out of sight under the metal railing to the trailer. Blade outward. That's how the Kowalski kid cut his hand—if he's telling the truth."

"Mel, you don't suspect him!" Jane exclaimed. "He's a bone-deep nice kid."

"You know him? Well?"

"Well enough. I only met him once, but he was nice to my cats. Stop giving me that look! I know it sounds stupid, but a person who is gentle and considerate to animals can't be a murderer."

"No? I was on a case once where the mass murderer fed his victims to his dogs."

"Oh, please—" Shelley said, turning away.

"Sorry. I shouldn't have said that. I'll take note of your evaluation of Butch Kowalski, Jane. Now, I have an important question for you."

He picked up the big manila envelope he'd put on the coffee table when he came in. He opened the end of it and very carefully pulled out a plastic bag. Inside was a blood-encrusted knife. "I'm sorry, Jane, but you must look carefully at this. Have you ever seen this knife before?"

Jane didn't answer for a long moment. Not because she didn't know the answer, but because she hated having to say it. Finally, she cleared her throat and said, "Yes, it's mine."

——10——

"How can you be so sure?" Mel asked. He sounded as if he was giving her every opportunity to change her mind.

Jane would have loved to take the admission back, but couldn't. "The kids gave me the set last Christmas. There are four and they go into a sort of chopping block thing. I accidentally set this one on a hot burner and part of the handle melted a little. See those two burner marks? And then Mike took it to his room to open a box and it hung around up there and got some green model airplane paint right where the blade fits into the handle. You can see a little of it."

"Are you okay, Jane?" Shelley asked.

"Yes. Just a little woozy feeling. Mel, please put it away."

"Sure. I'm sorry. You hadn't missed it when you cleaned up the mess in your kitchen?"

"No, why should I? I wasn't taking inventory and haven't even finished cleaning up. And even if I had noticed it wasn't in the block with the others, I'd have just assumed it was in the dishwasher or with the stuff I shoved into the guest bath."

"Do you remember where you last had it?" Mel asked.

"Mel, I don't pay that kind of attention to every kitchen utensil. Now, if you wanted to know the last time I hauled out the pasta maker or the cookie press or the electric meat slicer, I could probably tell you. But an everyday kitchen knife—? No. It's like an extension to my hand. I use it without even thinking."

She heard the sound of her own voice rising toward hysteria and took a deep breath, turning away to study the view out the window while Mel rattled around putting the gory knife back into the envelope. It was starting to get dark, but the movie production showed no signs of slowing down.

"This Kowalski person you mentioned is Jake's assistant, right?" Shelley asked Mel. "Why do you think he's lying about cutting his hand by accident?"

"I don't necessarily think he's lying," Mel said, putting the envelope next to the sofa out of sight. "I'm just saying it's possible. If he stabbed Jake Elder and in the process cut his own hand, he might have shoved the knife into the railing in order to make another explanation for his injury."

Jane had pulled herself together. "Even so, and putting aside my own impression of Butch, why would he kill Jake? Jake was his mentor, his employer."

"Protégés have knocked off mentors before, Jane," Mel said. "Sometimes that's how they get to be mentors in their turn. Or, suppose this: Butch had made some screw-up that Jake was not only going to fire him for, but bad-mouth him throughout the business. I get the impression from talking to people that Jake Elder knew everybody who was anybody and was well thought of—professionally, at least. I haven't met anybody yet who makes any pretense of having liked him."

"But what kind of mistake could Butch have made that would be that important? He was an apprentice, just a glorified gofer, it seemed to me. Learning the ropes from the bottom up by fetching and carrying."

Mel gestured toward the window and the scene beyond. "What kind of mistake? I'd think there'd be about a hundred you could make out there. Just look at all those electrical wires, for one thing. Those look like a disaster waiting to happen."

"But Jake and Butch had nothing to do with that part of it, did they?" Jane asked. "What could you do wrong with a prop that would matter?"

"I'm just speculating, Jane. It's my job," Mel said tightly.

"I know. I'm sorry. But Mel, you saw Butch at my kitchen table. Poor kid was about to faint at the sight of his own blood. Can you really imagine him doing something awful like that to somebody else?"

Mel shrugged. "Maybe that's what he was really faint about. Nobody saw his 'accident' with the handrail. We only have his word."

Shelley had been listening silently. Now she spoke. "Mel, tell us more about Jake's death. Where did he die? Was there a struggle? Did it take a lot of strength?"

"It doesn't look like it took strength as much as luck to slip the knife right between the ribs," Mel said. "He was apparently inside the props trailer, bent over slightly, looking into a crate. The blow was probably delivered downward, almost certainly by a right-handed assailant. The blade almost certainly pierced the back of his heart. At least that's what it all looked like at the scene. The lab work may show something else, but I doubt it."

"So anybody could have done it," Shelley said.

"Anybody at all," Mel agreed. "It was easy and clean. No blood spatters to speak of. No struggle. There was a cleaning rag with blood on it on the ground near the handrail, suggesting that the assailant probably wiped the fingerprints off the knife handle and maybe held it with the rag to jam it into the underside of the railing."

"I can't picture what you're talking about . . . this railing," Jane said.

Mel grabbed a newspaper off the end table and sketched. "The stair rail itself is just a thin piece of metal running along the top of the uprights. There's an upside-down U-shaped piece that fits over it to make a smooth handhold. But the underneath part of the U is open. And about the width of the knife handle."

"But who would notice that?" Jane asked.

"Somebody who was familiar with the trailer," Mel said. "Like Butch. But to be fair, anybody might have noticed. If you were going up the steps, holding the knife in your right hand and also steadying yourself with the rail, you might be aware that your fingers were curling into a place about the size of the knife."

"Why did the knife have to be hidden?" Shelley mused. "I suppose just because the murderer didn't want to be seen carrying it around. But why not just drop it in the truck?"

Mel shrugged. "I have no idea."

"Have you interviewed Butch?" Jane asked, wondering why she was feeling so protective of the boy. She supposed it was because she'd seen an intrinsic gentleness and vulnerability in him. Or perhaps after Mike's bad experience earlier in the day, her maternal instincts were just working overtime.

"Not yet. He's really pretty much of a mess. Scared to death of the responsibility that's fallen on him, he says."

"What responsibility?" Shelley asked.

"Apparently they only have a few days' filming left and the producers sent word that they don't want to bring in a new property master at such a late date. They want Butch to take over and see it through."

"—thereby making or breaking his reputation as a skilled expert in his own right," Jane finished for him. "Which might have been a motive. I see it in theory, but I don't believe it for a minute. If you'd seen how nice he was to—"

"—your cats. Yes, I know. Speaking of which, isn't that one of them?"

Mel pointed out the window where several people were trying to catch Meow and remove her from the craft service table, where she was browsing through the food.

*   *   *

"That explains the mess in your kitchen," Shelley said when Jane came back inside with a cat under each arm. She'd carried them through the kitchen where Mel was using the phone and the other long-suffering police officer was still interviewing cast and crew members.

"What does?" Jane dropped the cats and they sat looking up at her expectantly. "As if I've ever fed them in the living room," Jane groused.

"The knife," Shelley said. "Somebody needed a weapon that wouldn't be missed immediately, so they trashed your kitchen in the hopes that you wouldn't notice it was gone. Which is exactly what happened."

"Whoever it was obviously has no idea of my housekeeping," Jane said. "Even if I had missed the knife, I wouldn't question it. I lose things all the time. And the kids take them for projects." She paused, thinking out just how to express a thought that was troubling her. "Shelley, it makes me furious that somebody 'invaded' my house at all, but absolutely livid that they did it in order to get a weapon to kill somebody with. I'm outraged at being made a part of this, even a small part."

"But you aren't a part of it. The knife was just an object that happened to be in your house."

"I know that, but I'm still angry. And it's screwed up my whole week. I was all prepared to be the guilty mother and cook a series of extraordinary dinners for my children before going off on my weekend of sin."

Shelley grinned. "I hope this weekend can live up to your expectations."

"But I can't even cook now! The kitchen is full of police."

"That's fine," Shelley said. "Paul's gone and I was going to get Kentucky Fried for my kids. We can just get more and all eat it at my house."

"I don't know about that. Katie's social studies class watched a horrible documentary about chicken processing and she doesn't consider them politically correct. The only kind she'll eat is 'free range.' That sounds to me like some tough old bird you'd run over in Arizona. I didn't mind veal going out of style; I could never afford it anyway, but I hate losing chicken."

"Then how about carryout Chinese? Nobody can tell what's in Chinese food."

"Can I have a whole order of crab Rangoon to myself?"

"To eat, or to apply directly to your thighs?"

"Are we having Chinese tonight?" Mike said from the doorway.

"Mike! I didn't hear you come in," Jane said as Mike and his younger brother Todd came into the living room and took up positions peering out the back window.

Todd was making repressed jabbing motions. "We're practicing being burglars," Todd said. "What are they doing out there?"

"I have no idea," Jane admitted. "How was the movie you went to?"

She regretted having asked this, as she was treated to a blow-by-blow description of the martial arts film they'd seen. Todd enthusiastically demonstrated some of the better kicks and punches, almost knocking over her best lamp. Willard loved the performance, but the cats disappeared in the face of the violence and even Shelley tiptoed away, mouthing "One hour" as she went.

"It was great, Mom!" Todd finished up. "Is that the kind of movie they're making in the backyard?"

"No! Certainly not."

"I'm going to go call Elliot," Todd said. As he got to the doorway, he stopped. "Oh, yeah. Mike says you're going to New York this weekend. Could you get me some baseball cards? I'll make a list of what I want."

"Sure," Jane said weakly. When he was out of earshot, she said to Mike, "Does he know I'm going with Mel?"

"Sure. I didn't know you hadn't told him yet or I wouldn't have said anything."

"How'd he take it?"

"Fine, Mom. Don't worry."

"And you, Mike. How are you taking it?"

Mike smiled sheepishly. "Well, to tell the truth, I didn't much like the idea at first. My own mom, going off and shacking up with some guy. It didn't seem like a 'Mom thing.' But I didn't pay much attention to the movie this afternoon. I just sat there in the dark and thought about—about Dad and things. I guess it's pretty easy to think that somebody dead was perfect. And I hadn't really been remembering him. I'd been remembering, I dunno, I guess what I wanted him to be like."

"That's probably okay," Jane said softly.

"Yeah, for me. But not for you. You've been letting us think he was completely cool and all that time you must have really had your feelings hurt— like I did today."

Jane felt tears welling in her eyes. This was one *terrific* kid.

Mike saw the tears and started talking briskly. "So anyhow, I was thinking about it and decided why shouldn't you have a boyfriend? And why shouldn't you get to go on a trip with him if you want? You're a grown-up."

"Not nearly as grown-up as you think. I haven't told Katie either. Or your grandmother Jeffry."

Mike smiled. "I'll tell Katie if you want me to, but Gramma's your problem. Jeez! She's gonna go ballistic! I hope you'll let me hang out nearby when you tell her. I might invite Scott over to watch, too."

"Mike, I can't tell you what it means to me that—"

"Aw, Mom. Don't get mushy," Mike said, moving away before she could hug him. One hug a week was already beyond his limit. "If you'll give me money to put gas in the car, I'll pick up dinner."

——11——

"What are you looking so gloomy about? The food wasn't that bad," Shelley said when they were through eating.

The kids had gone into the living room to play with the Nowacks' new Super Nintendo. Outside in the near darkness the last of the movie people were finally clearing out after a thirteen hour workday. Shelley and Jane were looking over the wreckage of dinner. There were at least a dozen little white cartons with dabs of leftovers in them. Shelley set out three covered glass dishes. "All rice in one, all fried stuff in another, and everything else in the last one," she instructed as she set about loading plates and silverware into the dishwasher.

"Mel called just before I came over," Jane said. "I told him I'd had a talk with Mike and things were sorted out so that I could still go with him this weekend. I told him about my conversation with Mike, including the part about Steve leaving me. I'd never mentioned that to him before. I guess I was afraid of him knowing I was a reject."

"And . . . ?"

"And I was sorry I'd talked about it on the

phone. I wanted to see his face. He was real non-committal and cool. For all I know, he already knew about it. I had to tell the police where Steve was going that night, so it's in a report he could look up if he wanted."

Jane's mature son's voice wafted in from the living room saying, "Use your Moon Sword, butt breath!"

Jane shook her head in dismay. "Mike's walking a thin line between kid and adult and I never know which side he's going to slip over. I guess he doesn't either . . ."

"Jane! About Mel?"

Jane studied the last crab Rangoon, wondering if she could eat it without blowing up and decided she couldn't. "He said that was too bad because now he couldn't go because of this murder."

"Why not? There are other detectives who could take over," Shelley said.

"I know. I asked that too and he said since he was the person who actually found the body, he couldn't unload the case on somebody else. He was sounding cranky, like it was my fault he found the body."

"Jane, if he can't get away until this is solved, it could be months. You know how slowly the police work. Lab results alone can take weeks."

"I know." Jane dumped a half carton of shrimp fried rice into the proper bowl. "But there's nothing I can do about it."

"Except solve it for him," Shelley suggested.

"Shelley, you know how it pisses him off for us to butt in."

"Yes, but unless you want to take a walker and a case of Geritol along on your weekend of sin, we'd better."

"I don't know, Shelley. Those people might as well come from another planet for all we know about their lives. It's such a weird world they live in. We have no idea what makes them tick."

"They're still people, Jane. Same motivations as anybody else, just different frills." She started rinsing out empty paper cartons and putting them in the trash masher.

"You clean your trash before you throw it away?" Jane asked in wonder. Shelley was, hands down, a better housekeeper than Jane, but this surprised her.

"Sometimes. The masher takes so long to fill up that things can get awfully ripe. Somebody once told me a trash masher was the greatest invention in the world for turning fifty pounds of trash into fifty pounds of trash."

"No, the greatest invention this century is the hot glue gun," Jane said. "Everything from my dishes to my carpeting is held in place because of it. I keep hoping to find a way to use it on my hair."

"Come on, Jane. Don't change the subject. You know I'm right about the movie people."

"But it would mean hanging around them and frankly, my one lunch with them was a heart-stopper. I don't want to repeat that experience."

"But you won't. You got the shocking part over with right away, unless you think the other women on the set are going to be lining up to tell you they slept with your husband—which, I have to admit, is sounding like a possibility. Besides, they're interesting in their weirdness. And the one thing they seem to love above all else is talking about themselves."

Jane was beginning to feel a spark of hope. "You really think—?"

"I *know* we can get to the bottom of this before Mel can pick his way through DNA samples and fingerprints and heaven knows what else. You know it, too."

Shelley glanced around the kitchen for anything else that could go into the dishwasher and, satisfied there was nothing hiding, closed the door and punched the buttons to start it. Then she got a fresh pot of coffee started. As the dishwasher swished and hummed, she washed off the kitchen table, then sat down. "Now, it's simple, Jane. Somebody killed Jake. We just have to figure out why and who."

"Oh, sure. That *is* easy," Jane said.

"Sarcasm is wasted on me. It can't be that hard. Killing somebody isn't a normal way of dealing with problems. It's so abnormal that it ought to stand out a mile if we really concentrate on the problem."

"Okay, I'm concentrating," Jane said.

In the living room Shelley's daughter Denise shrieked with delight or defeat.

"Hold it down," Shelley shouted back.

"If I ever get to go away with Mel, I think I'll buy my kids the Super Nintendo to keep them busy while I'm gone," Jane said.

"You mean, to play with it yourself when you get back," Shelley guessed accurately.

"Okay, okay. Who killed Jake? I think the 'why' has to come first, don't you? And the obvious 'why' is the blackmail. We know he was attempting to blackmail at least one person and maybe others as well."

"Hold it," Shelley said. "Let's examine that. Do we *know* it was Jake doing the blackmailing?"

Jane considered. "No, not a hundred-percent sure. But if you know somebody was being blackmailed and a few hours later there's a dead body, can't you assume he was the blackmailer?"

"Okay, you're probably right. Tell me again what you heard."

Jane closed her eyes and tried to tune out the other noises to recapture the aural memory. "The first person, let's say 'A,' said something about being in a hurry. Then 'B,' who was probably Jake, said that girl had come down with chicken pox— no, I don't think he actually mentioned chicken pox. Just that somebody had come down with something. And then he said that 'A' knew what he wanted."

"But he didn't specify what it was?"

"No. It must have been something they had talked about before."

"Or something 'A' could be expected to know about him."

"Like what?" Jane asked.

"I don't know . . . like, maybe they'd worked together before and 'A' knew that Jake was terrified of diseases and would want to be excused from the set or something."

"Pretty thin," Jane said.

"It was the best I could do on the spur of the

moment," Shelley said, looking impatiently at the burbling coffeemaker. Shelley firmly believed she couldn't think without regular infusions of coffee.

"Okay, I'll go along with it provisionally. So Jake, if it *was* Jake, wanted this 'A' person to intervene with the director. They talked about Roberto. 'A' said he and Roberto were hardly on speaking terms and he couldn't and wouldn't help. And then 'B' started talking about what I supposed were dirty movies."

"So did 'A' agree to do whatever he was supposed to do?"

"No, I don't think so. That was the end of it. Jake must have moved away because 'A' just mumbled 'son of a bitch' and I didn't hear any more."

The coffeemaker had finally finished. Shelley got up and poured them both enormous mugs. "Don't worry. It's decaf," she said, handing one to Jane. "Okay. That's all we've got to work with. You think they were men's voices. Both of them?"

"I think so. But I can't be positive. And you heard me telling Mel that there was nothing unusual about their word choices or accents or anything."

"So, we have to assume this 'A' person was probably an actor rather than a technical person, right?"

"I think so," Jane said, blowing on her coffee. "I guess making porn films could reflect badly on a director, but probably not on anybody else."

"And we know it wasn't Roberto because 'A' had no accent and they were talking *about* him."

"Uh-huh. And it was probably an important actor, rather than somebody with a bit part."

"How do you figure that?" Shelley asked.

"Only because somebody in a minor part wouldn't be expected to have any influence on the director. Although, 'A' said he and Roberto couldn't stand each other."

"All this sounds to me like it must be George Abington."

"Yes, I'm afraid so."

"Why 'afraid so'?" Shelley asked.

"Because he's nice. He was the only one at the lunch who was polite to me. The only one who even acknowledged that I was there at all."

"How did he act toward Jake?"

Jane shrugged. "Nothing. No animosity, no friendliness. Nothing."

"He ignored Jake?"

"Not aggressively ignored. They just didn't happen to speak to each other. Well, nobody got to speak much because Roberto Cavagnari was holding forth."

"That seems strange. If somebody had tried to blackmail you and threatened to ruin your career, could you sit down with them an hour or so later and show no signs of anger?"

"Not unless I were a very good actor," Jane said.

Katie came into the kitchen. "Boys are so *dumb*," she said, as if it were a revolutionary discovery. "I'm going home, Mom. Thanks for a great dinner, Mrs. Nowack."

"Homework?" Jane asked.

Katie rolled her eyes. "Jeez, Mom. Like you have to remind me?"

"No phoning until it's done," Jane said.

From Shelley's side door she could see into her own kitchen. The police officer was still at the table, shuffling paperwork, so she felt it was all right to let Katie go home without escort. When Katie had gone, Jane went into the living room to question Todd about homework. When he admitted he had a few math problems to do, she sent him home as well.

When she rejoined Shelley, her friend was deep in thought. "Jane, suppose you turn this around."

"How?"

"Well, suppose Jake was the one being black-mailed instead of doing the blackmailing?"

"I don't follow you."

"Well, if somebody tried to blackmail Jake, and he thought about it and went back to the person later and said, 'I'm not doing what you want, and what's more, I'm going to 'fess up publicly to the porn movies and tell everybody what a slimeball you are—?' "

"Hmmmm. Seems a stretch to me," Jane said. "Maybe. But the blackmailer was talking about awards and how they don't give awards and honors to people who have been in skin flicks."

"But there are awards for technical things, not just acting," Shelley said. "And we don't know that Jake never acted. Or let us say 'performed' in naughty movies. I don't know that it requires any acting skill. He was certainly good-looking enough to be in front of a camera."

"So you're saying an intended blackmail victim might turn the tables and become the murder victim? Would that apply to George Abington? I'm getting confused. What would anybody want Jake to do for them?"

"Any number of things, I'd guess. Jake was highly respected in the business, it seems. He might have influenced the director to change a scene and feature somebody else since the girl who was supposed to be in it had gotten sick. For all we know, somebody is furiously rewriting the script right now to feature George or practically anybody else."

"So it could have been somebody really minor, too. Another bit player who wanted a shot at stardom?"

"It's possible," Shelley said. "Here's another possibility. And you won't like it. What if Butch wanted something of Jake? Like a better credit at the end of the movie, or more control of the props decisions or something. He might try blackmailing Jake and Jake could have come back and said, 'I'm not going along with this and, what's more, you're fired and I'm going to ruin your name in the business.' That would make him a threat worth killing, wouldn't it?"

Jane was shaking her head. "This is too baroque for me. I don't even know who 'A' and 'B' are anymore. And there's yet another possibility that we haven't considered."

"What's that?" Shelley asked brightly.

"That the blackmailing attempt I heard had *nothing* to do with the murder. With that many egotistical, ambitious people around, there are probably half a dozen nasty things going on at any given moment."

Shelley was only momentarily discouraged. "Then we have a lot of snooping to do to find out what the other nasty things were, don't we? Set your alarm for six, Jane. We've got a busy day ahead of us."

12

"So are you going to marry Mel?" Katie asked as she stood at the window watching for her car pool the next morning.

"Marry?" Jane gasped, nearly choking on her orange juice. "I don't know. I guess Mike told you about my plans."

"Yeah, he said you didn't want to talk to me about it."

"It's not that I didn't want to. I just didn't know how."

"What do you think I am, some kind of . . . of *prude*?"

"There are worse things to be," Jane said, wondering how she could get control of this conversation. "So you don't mind if I go?"

"Mind? No. It seems kinda silly. I mean, you're almost forty years old, Mom. Isn't that pretty old for—you know? There's Jenny's mom. Gotta go!" she said, flying out the door.

Jane went to the living room and glanced out the window. Eight o'clock and the movie people were in full swing. She'd heard trucks arriving shortly before six, but contrary to Shelley's instructions, hadn't gone out to snoop. Now that the kids were all off to school, she still wasn't in any hurry. She sat down and turned on the television, letting the morning news wash over her while she smoked a cigarette. She was down to six a day now and had pretty much given up trying to quit entirely. Still, six a day was better than the pack and a half she'd gotten up to in the weeks after Steve's death.

The conversation with Katie had shaken her. She never felt fully in control as a mother, but in this situation she'd been put in the position of supplicant, wanting, if not approval, at least permission from her children to lead an adult life. Her discomfort came mainly from the fact that she was on shaky ground logically. She still felt duty-bound to uphold a high moral tone for them to emulate, and this included sexual abstinence. For teenagers. But not necessarily for her. And that's where the logic fell apart. She'd put herself into the old "Do as I say, not as I do" position, which she found very uncomfortable. *She* knew what the difference was, but couldn't find a way to explain it to Katie.

Her daughter was poised on the brink, hormonally speaking, of being a woman. She still had a lot to learn about life and people and especially herself before she should consider becoming involved sexually with anyone. Whereas Jane herself was feeling menopause breathing down her neck.

She suddenly imagined she could hear her mother's voice speaking to her. "Chickie, you're doing it again. You're thinking too much about things you can't do anything about."

Jane put out the cigarette, tidied up the kitchen, and finished dealing with the last of the kitchen trash in the guest bathroom. Then she fed the cats in the basement, where they would be locked in today with fresh kitty litter and a big bowl of water. She had enough to fret herself silly about without having to worry about their whereabouts, too. Mike had taken Willard out to his dog run early and the big yellow dog was already settled in by the dining room window to begin his daily watch for the mailman. Jane double-checked that the doors were all locked, put the key to the back door in her jeans pocket, and went outside.

Shelley was just approaching the house. "Jane, I was coming to look for you."

"I had to get the kids off and had a brief, shattering talk with Katie to recover from. What have you found out?"

"Nothing. I was waiting for you. We work best as a team. I did try to get Jake's maybe-girlfriend Angela to chat, but she seemed to consider me a nobody and a busybody."

"Well? Aren't you?"

Shelley laughed. "Probably. I've been talking to Maisie about her, about Angela I mean, and it seems she's a very ambitious young woman. I've got a plan to get her talking. You catch her attention any way you want and just go along with me. Here she comes again . . ." Shelley added, lowering her voice to a whisper as she led Jane to the lawn chairs still set up by the snack table.

"Oh, hello there," Jane said to Angela, wishing she'd had the opportunity to question Shelley about this "plan" of hers. "Why aren't you in costume today?"

Angela Smith was in jeans and a beautiful red sweater. Her gorgeous chestnut hair was in trendy disarray. She glanced briefly at Jane, then went back to dropping tiny marshmallows into her hot chocolate. "I don't have any scenes until this afternoon. I just wanted to be around to see scene sixty-three done," she replied in a perfunctory tone.

"You'll have to excuse Jane if she seems nosy," Shelley said. "She's a writer and you know how they are."

"A writer?" Angela's interest was piqued slightly. "What do you write?"

The honest answer would have been "The first 104 pages of a story that might, with enormous good luck, turn into a novel sometime within the next decade." But Jane didn't get a chance to say anything.

Shelley leaped in. "I'm sorry, Jane. I know I'm not supposed to talk about it, but I can't help myself sometimes." She turned to Angela and said confidentially, "Jane's not allowed to reveal her pseudonym. Contractual reasons, you know. But I think it's all right to tell you that she had two novels on the best-seller lists last year and then, of course, there are the scripts—"

"Scripts? Novels?" Angela said hungrily.

Jane smiled modestly at Shelley. "Now, now. You'll give me away if you're not careful."

"Would I have read anything of yours?" Angela asked. She pulled up a vacant lawn chair and sat down alarmingly close to Jane.

"Oh, I wouldn't know——"

"Rosamund Pilcher! I'll bet that's who you are. No, she's English, isn't she? Will you tell me if I guess?"

"No, I'm sorry. I really can't reveal any more," Jane said.

"——and these scripts of yours? Are they based on your own novels? Have any of them been produced?"

"Have any of them been produced?" Jane said archly to Shelley and they both laughed merrily at the absurdity of anybody asking such a naive question.

"Let's just say it's no coincidence that this movie is being made in Jane's backyard," Shelley said.

Jane gave her a "look-out-you're-going-too-far" glance, and said to Angela, "I'm not *officially* involved in this production at all. Really."

It was almost obscene the way Angela's thoughts chased each other greedily across her otherwise lovely face. *Here*, she was obviously thinking, *is somebody of power and influence who could not only get me a plum role, but maybe write one for me.*

"Tell me about yourself, uh . . . Angela, was it?"

"Angela Smith. Yes. How nice of you to know my name. And yours is . . . ?"

"Jane Jeffry. Legally, that is," Jane said with a coy laugh that caused Shelley to make a noise like a seal barking.

"Sorry," Shelley said. "I think I inhaled a bug."

Jane had to look away from her to keep from bursting into seal barks herself. "So, Angela, you don't look like you're too upset about Jake's death," she said, plunging into the heart of the inquisition.

Angela looked taken aback, but by now was so eager to ingratiate herself with Jane that she had to respond. "Oh, but I am. Jake Elder was a legend. The business just won't be the same without him."

"That's odd," Jane said. "That you'd see it in those terms, I mean. I had the impression that you had a more personal relationship with him."

"Oh, no," Angela said, tossing her hair. "Not that Jake didn't want it that way, but no. I had enormous respect for him, of course. You can't help but respect people who have mastered their craft—" A respectful, puppyish look at Jane with this pronouncement. "But there wasn't anything really personal between us. I believe Jake may have wanted—well, to help me along some. He felt I had talent, you see. And wanted to see me succeed."

"That's odd," Shelley said. "I thought I saw you having an argument with him yesterday."

Angela gave Shelley a look that ought to have made her skin come up in blisters. "It was just a little disagreement about his method," she said. "Nothing at all."

Jane got a faraway look. A faraway "scriptwriter" look, she hoped. "Disagreements are the heart of fiction," she said meaningfully. "The very bone and meat of stories. Tell me all about it."

Angela looked like a butterfly pinned to a board. "It was nothing, really. Jake just wanted to help me a little. There was another extra who was supposed to do a scene with Miss Harwell yesterday and she got sick. Measles or something. Jake thought it would be nice if I stepped into her place. I mean, I am here. It would save the producers time from auditioning somebody else. And I have had years of acting lessons, and—anyway, he was just telling me that he'd mentioned the possibility to a few people."

Jane and Shelley exchanged meaningful glances. This was probably what Jake was wanting the unknown blackmail victim to help with.

"I don't understand," Jane said. "Why would that be cause for a disagreement? I'd think you'd be grateful."

"Oh, I was grateful! Very grateful!" Angela all but shouted. "But I want to make it on my own, you see. By my own talent and skills."

"Come now, surely it doesn't hurt to have a 'legend' point those skills out to others, does it?"

Angela squirmed. "Well, I think he was a little—ah, forceful about it."

"Forceful?" Shelley asked serenely.

"Offensive, maybe," Angela allowed. "Well, you had to know Jake to understand, but he never did anything subtle. Not with people. With things, yes. He was great with things. You've never seen anybody pay such fanatic attention to detail. I was an extra on another film he did here last year and it was a period piece and there was luggage. You know, old suitcases with stickers on them like people used to collect? And Jake discovered that some of the stickers weren't from the right period. He stopped the whole production to get them paint-ed out. Now, you know nobody in the audience would ever notice a thing like that, but Jake did and he said he wouldn't have his name on a film that allowed something sloppy like that. He shut down production for a whole day to get it fixed right."

"That must have made him popular," Shelley said.

"No, not popular, but he was right. And he was meticulous about being right. That's what made his reputation so great. If a person takes that kind of attention with little things, you know they'll never make big mistakes."

Jane wasn't so sure she agreed with this, but didn't argue. Angela was obviously working at leading them off the scent and Jane wasn't to be deterred. "So he was great with things, but not with people, you said?"

Angela looked defeated. "Yeah."

"And what had he done regarding you that you objected to?" Jane felt she was stabbing another pin into this beautiful butterfly. But having come this far, they couldn't release her before she confirmed their suspicions.

Angela looked down at her cup of cocoa, the marshmallows now melted down into a repulsive skin on the surface. "He'd threaten people," she said softly. "He didn't say so exactly, but I could tell what he meant. He was such an overbearing turd when he wanted something."

"But he wanted it for you, not himself," Jane pointed out.

Angela laughed bitterly, looking ten years older than she had moments before. "Don't kid yourself. Jake never did anything for anybody without a payoff in mind. He thought he'd do me a favor and I'd fall into bed with him. And in the meantime, half the cast and crew would have hated *me* for this goddamned 'favor' he was supposedly doing me. Some fucking favor!" she said, bursting into tears.

13

Jane patted Angela's hand absently while Angela cried it out. Shelley leaned over and whispered to Jane, "Don't let her off the hook yet. Find out what he had over people."

Jane whispered back, "A little recess first."

Shelley nodded her agreement.

Angela was sniffling into a paper napkin. "I'm— I'm sorry. I didn't mean to—I wasn't—"

"It's all right," Jane said in her best motherly tone. "We artists often wear our hearts and emotions very close to the surface."

Angela clutched her hand gratefully. "You *do* understand! I knew you would."

"If you aren't in a scene this morning, what are you doing here?" Jane asked, shifting the subject.

Angela relaxed visibly. She sniffled a few more times and pulled herself together. "I came to watch Miss Harwell do the crucial scene when Dora— that's the character's name—comes back years later and meets the man who betrayed her years before. It's a make-or-break scene any actress would kill for, but be terrified of. Very emotional. Calls for enormous restraint without actually pulling back

106

and will take perfect timing. It's a long, complex scene with a lot of emotional shifts. I thought I might learn a lot from watching her. Whether she gets it right or wrong, there's bound to be a lesson in it."

"Do you think she will get it right?"

Angela thought a while before answering. "I don't know. She's done so many doggy films that she may have lost whatever magic she once had," she finally replied. Now that the subject had turned from her, she had a surgical coldness regarding another's performance.

"Why do you think she made those films?" Jane asked. She wasn't fishing for anything in particular, just trolling for facts and impressions.

"Drugs, I guess," Angela said. "People do a lot of really stupid things for drugs. Not only to get their hands on the money they need, but because it makes their judgment real bad. Who knows? She might have actually thought they were good films."

"She does a lot of drugs?" Shelley asked.

"Oh, not anymore!" Angela said. "Not with that dragon woman on her case."

"Olive Longabach? Wasn't that her name?" Jane asked.

"Yeah, I think so. I heard Miss Harwell went to one of those Betty Ford places and since then the keeper won't let her out of her sight. I think this is the first film she's made since they dried her out."

"How do you suppose she got cast for such a good role? I'd have thought her career was pretty much dead," Jane said, genuinely curious now.

"That's quite a mystery. Her *and* Cavagnari. You know he's never done anything but spaghetti westerns and some male adventure stuff. Made a ton of money on them. Big box office, but no respect. The critics think he's a joke. Everybody's wondering how he and Harwell got chosen for this movie. It would have been a great role for Glenn Close or Meryl Streep or even Jane Fonda, if she was still making movies. There are a lot of big box office stars of the right age who can still just barely pull off looking young enough for the early scenes. There was even gossip about Cavagnari really wanting Jennifer Fortin, but I guess he was so glad to get the job himself that he didn't dare push too hard for her."

"Jennifer Fortin?" Shelley asked. "Why is that name familiar?"

"Oh, Shelley. You know who she is. She's done a lot of little arty things and got an Oscar a year or two ago for that film about Catherine the Great that you and I went to see and liked so well."

"Oh, yes! She was terrific!"

"This is very odd," Jane said. "Why not get one of those actresses for this role?"

Angela shrugged. "Who knows?"

In the back of her mind, Jane sensed gears turning, but couldn't quite sense what it all meant. Still, she was sure it meant something. "Just what kind of movie is this? We can't tell from back here."

The moment the words were out of her mouth she suddenly remembered that she was supposed to be "unofficially" involved in it, but apparently Angela was so interested in expounding her own theories that she didn't notice this *gaffe*.

"Arty and commercial both. Everybody's always looking for the perfect mix. You know, *The Last Emperor*, that kind of thing. Not that this is on that kind of scale and budget, but you know what I mean. Something the critics and the public will like. It almost never happens, but it might with this one. And if it's a success, Cavagnari and Harwell will both have it made. As long as the luck holds for Harwell . . ." she added.

This rang a faint bell in Jane's mind. "Oh, yes. Somebody else said she'd been on bad luck sets. But nothing's gone wrong on this one, has it? Until Jake's death, I mean."

"Only that girl getting sick and somebody at the studio got a burn from a light. But that's normal stuff," Angela said. "But Jake's death—well, that's really beyond bad luck, isn't it? I mean, somebody killed him. It wasn't just one of those things that happen for no reason. Now, about those scripts of yours—"

Recess was over.

"Who did Jake talk about you to . . . when he was trying to help you get that speaking part?" Jane asked before Angela could finish her own question.

"I don't know exactly," Angela said. She was starting to get a bit truculent. "George Abington, I think. Maybe Miss Harwell. Cavagnari. Possibly the producers. He hinted that he knew who they were. I don't know who else."

"And what did he say to all these people?"

"Just that he thought I'd be good for the role that was left vacant." Angela was verging on snappish now. Jane sensed she couldn't string her along much farther.

"No, I mean what 'pressure' was he applying to them?"

"I don't know! You don't think he'd have told me any of his secrets, do you?"

"No, I guess not," Jane said mildly.

She asked Angela a few more innocuous questions to defuse the young woman's growing irritation, made a few vague half promises about keeping her in mind when she was working on the next script, then excused herself to go in the house and make an imaginary call to her agent.

As she expected, Shelley followed along a few minutes later. "I wonder," Shelley said, "if she realized she was providing herself with the perfect motive for bumping off Jake?"

"I thought about that, too," Jane said. "By trying to help her, thereby getting her into his bed, he was wrecking her fledgling reputation in the business. If she's ambitious and greedy enough to fall for that ridiculous story about me being a famous writer, and put up with what we put her through just to suck up to me, she might have been ambitious enough to kill Jake to keep him from messing up her life."

"—and was she telling us because she's dumb, because she's innocent, or because she's smart enough to play a double bluff?"

"I don't know."

"Excuse me a minute," Shelley said, heading for the guest bathroom just off the kitchen.

When she came back, Jane was at the kitchen table, sorting a load of socks and underwear she'd just brought up from the dryer in the basement. "I've been thinking, Shelley, about a couple things that are bothering me. One, there's this 'bad luck' thing. Why would anybody have unfortunate things happen on a set just because they're there?"

"I guess that's the nature of bad luck," Shelley said, picking up a pair of socks and making them into a neat ball. "It just happens for no reason."

"I know. But having a murder on the set! That's about the worst luck I can think of. As much as I hate to admit it, it clears Harwell as a suspect in my mind. If she's the one who's had to fight the reputation for bringing misfortune along, she'd hardly be the one to create the worst misfortune of all, would she?"

"No, but we don't know what sort of provocation she might have had. There are lots of things worse than being considered a jinx."

Jane went on sorting and Shelley continued turning socks into balls for a few minutes. "I'm also curious about the mysterious producers. I don't know how on earth that could connect with a murder, but it is odd."

"Maybe it's not as odd as it seems to us. Way back when Paul was starting the fast-food outfit, there were a couple of people who were willing to invest in him, but didn't want anybody to know they were doing it." Shelley's husband had built up one tiny, floundering Greek food restaurant in the heart of Chicago into a nationwide chain in a little over twenty years.

"Why not?" Jane asked.

"Paul never knew. They just wanted it kept secret and he needed the money to get started and didn't question them. Nobody asked him to do anything illegal, so it didn't matter to him. It might have been some kind of tax dodge or hiding money to keep from paying alimony or anything. Maybe it's the same thing with this. And we don't know anything about the film business, Jane. Maybe it's common."

"Still, it is a secret and secrets seemed to be Jake's special interest."

Jane gathered up an armload of the sorted laundry. "I'll be right back." As she headed for the stairs, she stopped and looked back. "Shelley, a horrible thought just struck me. We've mentioned this before but haven't considered it as carefully as we should have. What if this blackmail had nothing to do with Jake's death? Maybe the whole crew was being blackmailed, but somebody killed him for some other reason entirely?"

——14——

Shelley's outrageous lie about Jane's being a famous writer must have spread. Angela apparently didn't mind sharing the news. When Jane went back out in the yard—minus Shelley, who had an errand to run—wondering how she'd get anybody else to speak to her, she found George Abington looking for her.

"Mrs. Jeffry, do you have a minute to talk?" he asked.

"Uh—sure."

"Let me get you a cup of coffee or a soft drink. Which do you want?"

"If there's an RC over there, I'd be grateful to get my hands on it," Jane said.

George rejoined her with her request and sat down next to her in Shelley's lawn chair. He was in costume, and made-up to look much older than he'd looked the previous day. Actually, he was made-up less, to look his real age. He wore graying muttonchop whiskers, a very realistic mustache, and a stiff-collared, turn-of-the-century suit. He must not have been wearing the punishing underwear because he had a bit of a paunch today. He looked like a prosperous Victorian banker. He sat down very carefully to avoid wrinkling the suit and set his hat down on the grass beside the chair.

"I hear you're a very successful scriptwriter," he said bluntly. "I just wanted to ask you to keep me in mind for a role. I know the writer doesn't always have any say-so in casting, but suggestions that a role was created with a certain actor in mind can't hurt."

Jane liked this approach much better than Angela's oblique obsequiousness. "What kind of a role are you interested in?" she asked, feeling utterly at sea. If she *were* a famous writer—a fabulous leap of imagination—would this be a logical question or was she blowing her cover?

"Anything. Anything at all to pay the taxes and mortgage," he said cheerfully.

"You can't mean that. Even a villain?"

"I'd be a hunchback child molester if the money was right," he said, then laughed at her surprised expression. "I don't know how many actors you know well, Mrs. Jeffry, but I'm the plumber kind."

"What does that mean?"

"Look, if I were a plumber, would I set myself up to only work on houses I felt were beautiful or had a sensible floor plan? Or worth more than X number of dollars? No. I'd work wherever I'd get paid. Same if I worked in a department store. I wouldn't say to a customer in the suit department that I didn't think his shape would do the reputation of my line of men's wear any good. I'd sell him the damned suit if he wanted it. Same with acting, in my mind. I'm an actor; that means I act. And if it means acting the part of a bartender with a facial tic, or a leading man, it's all the same to me."

"Well, that's a refreshing attitude."

"Not really. I think most people in the business feel that way, they just don't admit it. They dress it up in artistic crapola—you know, 'The role was small, but it gave me insights into the mind and soul of a waitress.' " He said this in a mocking voice surprisingly like Lynette Harwell's. "That's bullshit. Nobody can understand anybody else's soul. You just have to learn the lines and say them the way the director tells you to."

"What if you've got a lousy director?"

He shrugged. "Then you get a lousy movie. There's lots of those. But lousy or not, I've paid my kids' school fees, so what do I care? You'd be amazed how many rich actors there are that you've never heard of. Sometimes the really bad roles pay the best."

"You've got kids?" Jane asked, surprised. She'd never thought about any of these people being parents. Or going to the bathroom or doing anything else ordinary and human.

"Sure. I've even got a grandchild. A gorgeous little girl named Georgina, for me. Wish I had a picture along to show you. She's a doll."

"I'm confused," Jane said. "These aren't Lynette Harwell's children, are they?"

"Lynette? Have a baby?" He laughed. "No. Lynette wouldn't ever share a spotlight with a child, much less risk getting stretch marks. She'd have been the kind of mother who would make Joan Crawford look like Mother Teresa."

He shifted around getting more comfortable, apparently happy to settle in for a long chat. "No, these children are from my first marriage. My wife was a dress extra and I was playing one of sixteen thousand Roman legionnaires in an old epic. Just a couple dumb kids, although she wasn't half as dumb as I was. Now Ronnie's a fat granny married to a retired dentist in Encino. He was an orthodontist to stars' kids and made a bundle. Ronnie still keeps a hand in the business, but not as an actress."

"But you *were* married to Miss Harwell, weren't you?"

"For about a minute and a half. We weren't together long enough to even use up the leftover wedding cake in the freezer before she'd gotten her claws into Roberto. And he didn't last much longer."

"Isn't it awkward working with them?"

Someone walking by him tripped and sloshed some coffee. George quickly picked up the costume hat he'd set down next to the chair and checked it for spots. Satisfied it was unharmed, he said, "Not for me. Roberto's unhappy with it, but that's his problem. He hates me. I think he feels that I deliberately unloaded shoddy goods on him. It *wasn't* deliberate, but she sure is shoddy."

"You really dislike her?"

"Mrs. Jeffry—"

"Jane. Please."

"Jane, in a business that attracts and creates gigantic egos, hers towers over everyone else's.

She's truly the only totally self-absorbed person
I've ever known. To the point of psychosis, I
believe. If you asked her what a mailman does
for a living, she'd say he brings her mail. It
would never cross her mind, such as it is, to
imagine that anyone else *gets* mail, except those
few she might write to. I honestly believe she'd
have trouble understanding the truth if you told her.
She must know there are millions of people in the
world, but to her they're divided into fans of hers
and those half dozen pseudo-people who aren't. I
blame Olive as much as anybody."

"Olive? The older woman who's always with
her?"

"Yes. Poor old Olive is both the perpetrator and
the victim of the Ego That Ate the World. Lynette
treats her like shit, but Olive seems to thrive on
it. Do you know, when Lynette and I were first
married, Olive actually expected to sleep in the
room with us?"

"You're kidding!"

"I'm not kidding. And it gets worse! Lynette
couldn't quite grasp why I objected," he said, shaking his head in wonderment. "I got Olive out of the
bedroom, but I always suspected she was sleeping
across the doorway in the hall, like a medieval serf.
She was an actress herself once. Not a very good
one, I'd guess."

"I can't imagine that."

"Lynette told me she was, but it is hard to picture. If I'm remembering right, she was one of
those 'born in a trunk' kids. Too late for vaude-
ville, of course, but the parents were in some kind

of touring company—a country and western road show maybe—and dragged her around, sticking her in their act, until she was a teenager, then she got away from them by becoming a nanny to Lynette's family. Lynette's mother was one of those real remote high-society types who only wanted to see the kids all spiffed up for five minutes before dinner and it was Olive who filled Lynette's mind with the idea of acting. Olive found the teachers, took her to dancing lessons, made sure she got braces on her teeth, harassed the booking agents, set up her retirement fund for all I know. And created an egomaniac. Oh, well. To each his own, I guess."

Interesting as this might be, it wasn't shedding light on the immediate problem. "So, you've played all kinds of roles then?" Jane asked.

"Just about anything you could imagine," George answered easily. "College profs, garbage collectors, sheriffs—"

"What about porn movies?" Jane asked quickly before her nerve failed.

George's head snapped around and he stared at her for a long minute before saying, with a laugh, "So the lurker's been gossiping to you!"

"Lurker?"

"Yeah, whoever was eavesdropping on Jake and me told the police and I guess is spreading the word far and wide."

Jane prayed her face wasn't as red as it felt. "Oh, surely not," she said.

"Don't be embarrassed about knowing," George

said in a kindly manner that made Jane feel even worse. "It's not something I take out billboards about, but it's not such a deep secret. Sure, I did a couple porn movies way back when. My wife had some kind of expensive female troubles after our second kid was born and we were on the brink of welfare. It was a job. And my wife approved. She even vetted the contracts. She was always good with stuff like that."

Jane decided, since she was playing the innocent, she might as well play it for all it was worth. "What do you mean about Jake? What's Jake got to do with it?"

"Jake was trying to blackmail me. Stupid waste of time, but Jake was good at wasting time."

"Blackmail you into what?"

"Into trying to get that little chippy Angela Smith into a scene with Lynette and me. As if Roberto would care what I wanted. Ridiculous. Jake was really scraping the bottom of the barrel when he got to me."

"Do you think he'd tried it on other people? The blackmail, I mean."

"If he had anything on them, yeah, probably."

"But you don't know who else he tried it on?"

"No idea."

"What did you mean about his wasting time?"

"Just that he has—had a reputation for being a niggling perfectionist. It was his gimmick. He's shut down work for hours getting some damned trivial piece of something exactly right and as often as not, it wasn't even in the frame anyhow, but it got everybody bowing and scraping to him as a master."

"So he wasn't good at what he did?"

"Oh, he was good all right. But no better than a dozen others in the business. He just invented this mystique about himself and a lot of people bought it. The more of a bastard he was, the more the 'legend' grew. Well, it worked for him."

"Angela believed in the legend."

"Well, she would. She's his niece."

"His *niece*!"

"Yeah, what did you think?"

"She said he was trying to seduce her."

George laughed. "Then that lie was the only good bit of acting she's ever done. Angela Smith's shoulder blades are rubbed raw from sleeping around. She's normally a hopeless excuse for an actress. My daughter took some acting lessons once and ol' Angela was in the class. Angela got to be a legend herself for sheer awfulness."

"I wonder what else she lied to me about—" Jane said.

She wasn't able to pursue this, however, as a production assistant burst through the "doorway" in the scenery just then and said, "Oh, Mr. Abington! I've been looking everywhere for you. Mr. Cavagnari wants you for a run-through. And Mrs. Jeffry, you can let your dog out now for"—she consulted her watch—"seventeen minutes."

Jane met up with Shelley while she was dragging Willard out to his dog run. "Learn anything while I was gone?" Shelley asked, pitching in and pushing on Willard's back end.

"Yes, that Angela Smith lied to us. At least George Abington says she did. Unless"—she looked up at Shelley—"unless George Abington lied to me, too."

——15——

As the morning wore on, the whole atmosphere seemed gradually to become electrified. A photographer from *People Weekly* magazine showed up with an assistant who was ruthlessly snagging people to interview, and a whole crew of individuals from "Entertainment Tonight" arrived on the scene and got underfoot in creative ways. These outsiders made a difference in the mood of the set. Crew members who had previously appeared practically comatose bustled around looking busy and vital. Grips hauled things about in an intense, frantic manner, calling out, "Look out! Coming through!"

Jane caught up with Butch Kowalski briefly when he was having a short break at the craft service table. "How's your hand?" she asked.

"I'd almost forgotten about it," he admitted. "It's fine." He was slathering mayonnaise on a piece of bread.

"You'll ruin your lunch."

"Oh, I won't have time for lunch today," Butch said, slapping slices of ham on the bread.

A young man suddenly yelled at him from the break in the scenery. Butch turned and watched the other young man make some gestures, then laid his half-constructed sandwich down and gestured back with his still-bandaged hand.

Jane watched this, fascinated. "What was that all about?"

"Huh? Oh, we're setting up for an important scene and Ted wanted to know about where to put some stuff."

"Who's Ted and why all this," Jane said, imitating Butch's hand motion.

"Oh, Ted's an intern. Getting school credit for helping Jake. Now for helping me. And the sign language is what Jake made everybody who worked for him learn. Cuts out a lot of yelling across the set. Jake hated yelling. He said it was an undignified way to work."

And that kind of attitude probably added to the "mystique" that George Abington was talking about, Jane thought. "How are you doing on your own?" she asked.

"Okay, I guess. Jake had everything laid out to the littlest detail, so I'm just following his directions, but it's kinda scary anyway. If there's something missing or wrong today, I'm in big trouble without Jake to tell me how to fix it."

"You'll do fine," Jane assured him.

He was gulping down the sandwich now, his mind obviously on the important work ahead, so she left him alone.

Jane looked around for Shelley, but couldn't spot her anyplace. Maisie, however, waved her over to where she was using an unexpected bit of leisure to rearrange her first aid kit. Maisie's springy dark hair looked electrified, but whether it was from the humidity or neglect, Jane couldn't guess. "Hi, Jane," she said, ticking off small boxes of gauze on a checklist.

"What's with everybody?" Jane asked. "There's suddenly a different mood."

Maisie finished her chore and closed the box her equipment was in. "Oh, partly it's the end of the film hysteria. It sometimes happens that way. But mostly it's because there's an important scene this afternoon that calls for everything in the book. Cameras panning on tracks, lots of extras, different scenery, possibly a special effect if the 'rain man' can get his rain machine fixed. There's some kind of problem with the hydrant the water's supposed to come from."

"So is that why the magazine and television people are here?"

"No, they're here on the scent of blood. Jake's. Hoping there might be a spectacular arrest. It's the one kind of publicity nobody wants."

"But I haven't even seen the police," Jane said, meaning she hadn't seen Mel all day even though she thought she'd noticed his little red MG parked way down her block. But with all the extras' cars clogging the street, she couldn't be sure.

"Oh, they're here in droves. Roaming around on the set, driving everybody mad. The police can't seem to grasp why everybody's going on with a silly movie in the face of murder and Roberto can't grasp why the police keep interfering in an important thing like a movie for something as trivial as murder. I wouldn't be surprised if Roberto doesn't end up in jail himself eventually on a charge of tangling the wheels of justice or something."

"Maisie, who do you think killed Jake?" Jane asked, imitating George Abington's apparent bluntness.

"I can't imagine," Maisie said, not the least surprised by the question. "I really can't. I don't know anybody who didn't find him offensive, but there's a lot of people in this business who make a life's work of being offensive and they don't end up murdered."

"But Jake was blackmailing people. That's a considerable step up from 'offensive.' "

"Was he really? I'd heard gossip this morning. To be honest, Jane, I don't put much credence in blackmail as a motive. Not with actors anyway."

"What do you mean?"

"Well, actors love to talk about themselves, get 'reputations,' be closely involved in scandals. Not all of them, of course, but most of them will tell you their life stories at the drop of a hat. They never get tired of hearing about themselves, even if it's from their own lips."

"So I've noticed."

"So it's hard to blackmail a performer. And especially so nowadays. It used to be that a charge or alcoholism or homosexuality could destroy a career, but these days it's the 'in thing' to share their most intimate secrets with the public. Anybody who's anybody has been in drug rehab. In fact, I understand there's quite a hierarchy of places to go for it. Some of the rehab units even have their own publicist handing out 'star-studded' lists of former patients."

"So is nothing worth keeping a secret?"

"You tell me. Willie Nelson has told the world about his tax problems. Everybody on the screen or stage wants to talk about their infidelities and brushes with the law."

"I guess you're right."

"Even the things they *haven't* done are on the front page of the tabloids and most performers seldom even bother to sue the rags. Sometimes they even have their staff plant the fake stories. I guess they figure any publicity is good publicity. Besides, Jane, the blackmail didn't work."

"What do you mean?"

"Angela didn't get the part. That's what the gossip mill says he was working on, getting Angela the vacant part yesterday afternoon."

"Oh, I found out something interesting about Angela. At least I think I did. George Abington says Angela was Jake's niece."

Maisie laughed. "Oh, was she?"

"George Abington says so. Do you suppose he's right?"

"I have no idea. Never met the man before. He could be a pathological liar for all I know. But— he could be right. I just assumed it was a romance from all the attention Jake paid to her, but it could have been plain old nepotism. Come to think of it, she looks sort of like him. The same coloring and the sharp planes of their faces. They could be related."

"But she told me he was trying to seduce her."

"That's when she was trying to impress you, right? I heard about you being a famous scriptwriter. That doesn't happen to be true, does it?"

"No, of course not. But it does make people talk to me. I didn't come up with it. Shelley did."

"Then that's why Angela lied. She was trying to get you to see her as the poor, virginal heroine and write her a tasty role."

A hand fell heavily on Jane's arm.

She turned and looked at Shelley, who was wide-eyed and stunned-looking.

"Shelley, you look like somebody just hit you with half a brick," Jane said. "Come sit down and tell me what's wrong."

They took up their positions in their lawn chairs. "I've been talking to Lynette Harwell. Or rather, I've been being talked at by her. I knew you wouldn't want to have a chat with her, so I gave it a shot."

"And . . . ?"

"And she's amazing. Amazing . . ." Shelley's voice trailed off as if she were remembering a horrible event from the distant past. Like the Black Plague.

"Shelley, get a grip!"

"Yes, yes. She ought to be institutionalized. She's not quite human. Jane, she knows and cares about positively nothing but herself. *Nothing*, I tell you! I asked her about other people in the cast and she quite honestly didn't seem to know who I meant. She seemed to dimly remember George Abington. Not because she was once married to him, mind you, but because she had some scenes with him.

I'm not kidding! George only exists, in her mind, to fill in spaces in the script with talk so that the camera can focus on her reactions."

Shelley was hanging onto Jane's arm, as if it were her last link with the real world.

"What about Jake?"

"She didn't seem to really know quite who he was. I asked her if she'd ever worked on a set with him before and she looked at me as if I were crazy to expect her to remember anybody she's ever worked with. Her only interest in Jake was that he 'got himself killed'—that I assure you is a direct quote—and has perpetuated the myth about her being bad luck on a set."

"No!"

"By that time I was so fascinated, that I asked her what she knew about his death and she knew nothing. Not that he was stabbed, or where or when it happened. I tried to make her speculate on who did it and she just said, 'Well, I didn't.' Understand this, Jane, that wasn't a denial of guilt, it was a statement that if *she* didn't do it, who could possibly have any interest in who did? Amazing."

"That all fits with what George Abington said about her. I'll tell you about my conversation with him in a minute. So you're pretty sure she was telling the truth? About not killing Jake?"

"Positive. When she ran out of self-praise for a second, I quickly asked her if Jake had been blackmailing her and she was genuinely astonished at the question. Blackmail, she explained rather patiently to me, requires that a person has done something wrong. She—it should have gone without saying—had never done anything wrong."

"But she was in drug rehab, wasn't she? Why didn't you bring that up?"

"Oh, I didn't need to. She did. She was put in some kind of institution. She went on about it until I was ready to throttle her," Shelley said. "I didn't exactly get the idea it was to do with drugs, but it was hard to tell. She's worked it around in her mind that she was merely there to brighten the days of the patients and staff. A charitable act, don't you see? She likened it to Dorothy Lamour handing out coffee and donuts at the U.S.O. during World War II. Although she didn't mention the war itself. I don't think she knows there was one. She hadn't been born yet, so what could there have been for people to fight about!"

"Shelley, if your voice gets any higher, only dogs and bats will be able to hear you! Calm down."

She sighed heavily. "I know. You think I'm exaggerating, but I'm not. All of this"—Shelley waved wildly, a gesture encompassing the whole set—"all of this is a waste of money. I tell you, that one good performance she gave so many years ago *was* a fluke. This is going to be a bomb of a movie. What I don't get is why anybody cast her in a supposedly good role. It couldn't have been anyone who ever spent five minutes with her. No wonder the producers are hiding! They must be the stupidest people in the world."

"But Shelley, when I overheard her talking to Mike, she was talking *about* him, not herself."

"No, Jane. She was talking about him in order to seduce him into thinking *she* was wonderful."

"True, I guess."

"And even when she was talking about your husband, she was trying to make herself look like a tragic heroine, but still generous and capable of recognizing talent. Think back, Jane. Wasn't that the case?"

Jane shuddered. "I don't want to think back on that conversation. Ever. Shelley, do you think maybe she's really crazy enough to have killed Jake and, well—not remember it?"

"Oh, I guess it's barely possible," Shelley said with resignation. "She's so far beyond my range of human experience, I couldn't even guess. For all I know, she's been knocking people off right and left and has justified it as Lady Bountiful sparing them the pain and indignity of growing old . . ."

Her voice trailed away and her eyes grew very wide again.

"Will you just look at *that!*" Shelley exclaimed.

——16——

"Good Lord!" Jane exclaimed. "Isn't that Jennifer Fortin? And we were just talking about her yesterday!"

A crowd of people were surrounding the willowy blond actress who had just arrived in Jane's backyard and was dispensing waves and smiles like royalty. "What's *she* doing here?" Jane asked.

"Just throwing a little shit at the fan," Maisie said from behind them. She pulled a chair up and sat down with a wicked glint in her eye. "I heard she was in town, but I never thought she'd show up here. What superb timing. She must have a mole on the set."

"What *are* you talking about?" Jane asked.

"You must not be up on your movie gossip," Maisie said, shaking her head. "Jennifer was rumored to want this role badly. And Cavagnari wanted her too, by all accounts. But Harwell got it, which must have made Fortin crazy. Fortin's gotten a little testy when interviewers have compared her performances to Harwell's one great one. I wouldn't think Harwell much likes it either, especially when the movie rags talk about how Fortin looks so much like a young Harwell. So here's Fortin, on the very day Harwell *has* to do her best work or write her career off. Dear Lynette is going to go haywire when she learns who's hanging around the set watching her today."

Jennifer Fortin was moving out of sight, surrounded by crew members and the *People Weekly* staff.

"How long has she been in town?" Jane asked.

"A couple days, I think. Why?" Maisie asked.

"Did she have any connection with Jake Elder?"

"Oh, I doubt—" Maisie started, then stopped abruptly. "Now that you mention it, it was Jake who said she was in town. The first day we were here. He was talking to somebody about having had dinner with her the night before."

Shelley looked grieved. "I sure wish you hadn't said that. All we need now is another suspect."

Mel Van Dyne looked like he'd been dragged through a hedge backward. It wasn't so much the physical appearance of his clothes or hair as a frenzied look in his eye.

"These people are nuts!" he said with disgust. "That—that *director*, the one wearing the green 'thing,' just snatched somebody I was questioning right away from me. Literally grabbed the guy's arm and took him off mid-sentence. We were playing tug-of-war with him!"

"Want to go inside and neck?" Jane asked.

It accomplished what she hoped.

He whooped with laughter. "I'd take you up on that any other time!" he said. "God! You're right.

I'm letting them get to me too much. I'm losing it. I would like to go inside. I need to use your phone if I could."

Jane tactfully disappeared into the basement to check that the cats hadn't found anything important to damage while Mel reported in to his office. Max and Meow were outraged at their confinement, but had done nothing worse than kick the kitty litter around the floor in a pretty wide circle.

When she came back up a few minutes later, she found Mel standing by the windows of her living room, staring at the scene behind the house and shaking his head.

"How's it going?" she asked.

He made a helpless gesture. "Miserably, if you really have to know. I've managed to find at least twelve people with seventeen motives. Some of them happily handed me two or three reasons they might have wanted to kill him— like they were giving me little presents. None of them very convincing reasons at that. I've never heard anything like it. And at least fifty people had the opportunity to kill him."

"I guess this means you're not going to have it all cleared up by Friday," Jane said wistfully.

"I don't often feel stumped, Janey, and I don't handle it well. Now they're all wound up like tops about other things and I can't seem to hammer through to anybody that there's been a goddamned murder here and it has to be solved!"

"What other things?"

Mel jammed his hands into his pockets glumly. "Oh, somebody had a lot of money stolen this morning. God knows why the idiot had all that cash—"

"How much?"

"Over a thousand dollars. In a canvas bag, left hung over a chair. Jeez! Stupid! Anyway, it turned up. But only after I had to divert two of my officers to look for it."

"Where did it turn up?"

"Rolled up in an empty coffee cup in the makeup trailer. Naturally, practically everybody in the cast and crew cheerfully admitted having been in the makeup trailer during the relevant times."

"The money was in plain sight?"

"Yes," he snapped. "In plain sight. Why?"

"No reason. It just sounds like somebody wanted to be sure it was found. It's strange."

"Strange? Strange! Have you personally seen or heard anything *normal* from these people?"

Jane didn't smile, but it hurt not to. She'd never seen him unravel like this, and while she was sympathetic, she was also pleased. Mel was always just a shade cooler and more composed than she might have wished. A tiny, unwanted element in their relationship was her constant feeling of ever-so-slight intimidation in the face of his careful self-control.

"Now—" he continued his litany of grievances, "they're gearing up for something terribly important this afternoon. Important to them, that is. It's just a movie, Janey! Don't any of them understand that?"

Jane thought about pointing out to him that it was their whole reason for being, just as solving crimes was his, but wisely refrained from making this observation. She also curbed her inclination to ask him again whether there was the slightest chance that they'd manage to get away for their weekend in New York. That wasn't going to happen.

Unless she and Shelley could figure out who killed Jake Elder.

She pushed the thought aside. For all her unofficial snooping, she wasn't any farther ahead than Mel and his staff. With some reluctance, she mentioned to him Jennifer Fortin's arrival on the set. "She knew Jake, too. Apparently had dinner with him the night before they started work here."

"Oh, great . . ." he said dismally.

When Jane got back outside, the same table was being set up in her backyard for luncheon. This time she avoided sitting at it, but instead she and Shelley took up a listening post nearby. A moment later Cavagnari swept into the area with Jennifer Fortin on his arm. They were both smiling and gently pawing each other. Jennifer hung on his arm, giving it little squeezes and hugs and he kept patting her cheek and making what he probably imagined were seductive expressions. In Jane's view, the green velvet poncho detracted considerably from his effort.

"If that isn't a love feast, I don't know one when I see one," Shelley murmured. Cavagnari and Fortin had seated themselves practically on the same chair and were feeding each other little tidbits of cheese cubes from a tray that had been set on the table.

Jane just shook her head in wonder at the spectacle.

"What has Mel found out?" Shelley asked quietly. "I saw you snag him and take him inside."

"Nothing. Poor Mel is going nuts. He's not cut out to deal with the artistic temperament."

"Who is?"

"Oh, you and I are much better equipped than he is. Anybody who's trying to raise teenagers without going to jail or the loony bin isn't too surprised by anything."

"I guess you know that the junior high was taking school pictures today," Shelley said.

Jane knew exactly what this seeming *non sequitur* meant. "Oh, no! That explains why Katie was made up like a floozy raccoon this morning. I wondered. What do you think would happen if I ran up to school, dashed into her math class, and washed her face?"

"She'd hate you," Shelley said simply. "I made Denise kill the hairdo this morning. She was wild. She had her bangs moussed into a three-inch crewcut. It was appalling. I tried to make her understand that school pictures are forever. They come back and haunt you when you're thirty-five. You know, sometimes I get tired of being a warden. I can't wait for her to grow up and get to be my friend. Do you think it will ever happen?"

Jane shrugged. "My mother always said that when your kids grow up they just get scarier, more expensive problems. Of course, she had to cope with my sister Marty marrying that jerk . . ."

"It's so frustrating, having Denise known far and wide for absurd hair, when she has so many good qualities I'd like to see immortalized instead. Maybe I could make her wear a placard around her neck that says, 'I'm very tidy and get straight A's.' Do you think people might read it instead of falling back in horror at her bozo hair?"

"Probably not."

"She was so cute when she was ten," Shelley mused. "I wish I could have kept her that way. Locked in amber or something. Her school picture that year was darling, she still liked me and her father. She even got along with her brother at that age. She didn't care about money yet. It was the last good year . . ." she said in a voice of doom.

Jane nudged Shelley out of her grim reverie.

"Uh-oh," Shelley said, the gloom deepening.

Lynette Harwell had just come through the break in the scenery and was taking in the spectacle of Jennifer Fortin and Roberto Cavagnari all but locked in a cheesy embrace. Her lovely face was suddenly transformed into a mask of anger, and just as quickly became bland. Her sense of theater, or self-glorification, came back. She might not have any real intelligence, but she knew better than to cast herself in a bad light.

"Jennifer Formas, isn't it?" she said in a sweetly trilling voice. "How nice of you to drop by."

"Why, Lynette Harwell! I didn't know you were in this film!" Fortin said, ignoring the fact that Harwell had deliberately gotten her name wrong. "Roberto, darling, you've been keeping secrets from me," she gushed.

"Hardly a secret, my dear," Harwell said. "But some of us keep in touch with the industry better than others. What on earth are *you* doing in Chicago? Are you doing a trade show or something?"

This dig must have been close enough to the truth to hurt. Jennifer's face wasn't quite as well controlled as Lynette's and she frowned slightly.

But before she could rally her forces and retort, Lynette cut her off. "Well, you must excuse me, darling. I have a terribly important scene this afternoon and really can't let myself get distracted by trivialities."

Shelley leaned close to Jane and said, "I make it 3–1 in favor of Harwell."

Jane giggled. "She's a real trouper, isn't she? Max and Meow could learn a few things about cattiness from her."

——17——

Lynette Harwell ostentatiously continued to study her script throughout lunch, with Olive hovering around, feeding her tidbits of lunch as if she were a baby bird and occasionally stabbing a long finger at the script and giving advice in equally tiny doses. It was the first time Jane could remember actually seeing a script in anybody's hand.

Jennifer Fortin continued to flirt halfheartedly with Cavagnari for a while, but when it became apparent that she wasn't going to get any more adverse reaction from Harwell, she abandoned the effort and started chatting with a hovering reporter. Cavagnari didn't seem to mind. He had become quiet and thoughtful, too, picking at his fried chicken and staring at nothing as if he were undergoing some kind of mental girding process. Even George Abington became uncharacteristically serious about his craft, asking Cavagnari some technical questions about lighting and positioning.

Finally, Cavagnari straightened up and said, "Let's do it!"

A production assistant who had been standing behind him in a state of suspended animation, shouted into his bullhorn, "Everyone on set!"

The behind-the-scenes area in Jane's yard was cleared as suddenly as if he'd shouted "Fire!" Within moments Jane and Shelley were left alone with Maisie. Half sandwiches were abandoned, cigarettes ineffectively stubbed out to smolder in sand-filled coffee cans, drinks set down anywhere close at hand.

"Wow!" Jane said. "Is this for Lynette's big scene?"

"Everybody's big scene, really. But mainly Lynette's," Maisie said.

"Do you think we could watch a little?" Shelley asked. "If we stayed out of everybody's way?"

"I imagine so. As long as Cavagnari doesn't notice you," Maisie said. "What you need to do is find the biggest, ugliest piece of equipment you can find and glue yourselves to it. If it's big, they won't want to move it capriciously or let it be in a scene."

They followed her advice and furtively perched on a big orange thing they decided might be a generator. It wasn't operating, so they felt it was safe to climb onto it. But they were disappointed at how little they could really see of the production, even from what should have been a good vantage point. There was a fairly large group in the scene. Lynette, George, and at least a dozen extras. But between Jane and Shelley and the actual scene were cameras, cameramen, reflectors, lighting equipment, sound equipment, and at least fifty technical people who were either standing around to watch or prepared to exercise their particular skills.

There was a lot of movement, but no distinguishable sounds from this distance; just a jumble of voices with the occasional sentence sticking out.

"Get that track back about a foot."

"Don't take it so fast. Stroll, don't walk!"

"That baby spot's flickering."

"I'm picking up a siren from someplace."

"Shit! A jet-trail."

"Oh, God! Get wardrobe! Her skirt's torn!"

"I don't know where I'm supposed to stand."

"A little louder, please."

"You're killing me, baby."

"Put a clamp on that thing."

"Can't do it that way. There's a telephone pole in the frame."

For all the hurry to get to work, it was at least a half hour before any noticeable— to Jane's eyes — progress was made. A production assistant said, "Rehearsing!" into a bullhorn and the technical people froze in place while the actors and extras walked through the scene. And walked through again.

And again. And again.

Cavagnari charged here and there, giving instructions, berating extras and crew members, dragging people to different positions, trying it out in various ways like a demented choreographer. When he had the movement of the scene down to his satisfaction, he started working on the lines and the timing of them.

Finally, the bullhorn voice said, "Quiet on the set!" and a moment later, "Rolling!" and they started to film. And it was as tedious and repetitive as the rehearsal. They did the whole scene with a camera at the left end and another in front of the principal actors. They did it again with a camera at the right end. Somebody flubbed a line. They did it again. Then they did the whole scene, which was quite a long one, with the camera running slowly along a track at the back of the set.

Twice during filming, a plane went over with a low hum that wouldn't have been noticeable otherwise and the sound people shouted, "Incoming!" and halted production.

Finally some of the extras on the fringes of the scene were released and they started filming it all over again close-up. They'd focus each camera on one person while the entire scene was played out, just getting the appropriate reactions on faces.

But Jane and Shelley couldn't hear a word of dialogue except for the one place where Lynette shouted, "But I trusted you!" Then she lowered her voice again. They heard this one line so many times that Jane finally couldn't stand it anymore. "I'm going back to my yard," she whispered to Shelley. "The kids ought to be home pretty soon."

Shelley nodded her agreement, and when they stopped filming the next time, the two women made a quiet, hasty retreat. Jane's backyard was still nearly deserted, but a couple of extras were standing by the big coffee urn. "So one actor says to another, 'How are things?' " one of the extras was saying, "And the other actor says, 'Oh, just awful. My agent came to my house and he raped my wife and killed my children and then burned my house down.' And the first actor says, 'Your *agent* came to your *house*?' "

They were still laughing as Jane went inside.

She quickly stirred up a premixed batch of brownies and set bananas and milk out on the kitchen table. She checked the mail, gave Willard a big pet and tried to explain to him why he couldn't go outside just now, and got the kitchen floor hastily mopped while the brownies were cooking. Just as she opened the oven door to remove them the kids started arriving, with Mike home first.

She was once again struck with how resilient kids are. As resilient as they are vulnerable. Mike had dealt with his distress of the day before and was back to being his normal self.

"Scott and I want to go to the library. Can I have the car for an hour?" he said, juggling a brownie that was still too hot to eat.

"I've never known you to be so eager to study," Jane said.

He rolled his eyes. "Mom, there's a new girl working there. We've just got to check her out. Check her out . . . get it?" He roared with laughter, exhaling brownie crumbs which Willard got before they hit the floor.

"Okay with the car, but stop and get some orange juice while you're out." Jane fished some cash out of her purse and gave it to him.

"Wow! Brownies! Cool, Mom!" Todd said a moment later as he dumped his backpack on the floor.

"Take that upstairs first," Jane said, holding the brownie pan out of his reach.

"Aw, Mom. In a minute. I'm starving. Hey, Elliot's uncle gave him his old stamp collection. Elliot says some of them are pretty cool. Can I go over there?"

"If you're home by five. Hey! Leave some brownies for Katie. Eat a banana."

"Katie's dieting," Todd said.

"I'll drop you off at Elliot's," Mike offered.

They each knocked back a glass of milk and grabbed a banana as they left.

Katie came in a minute later. The overdone makeup she'd started out with had smudged, making her look more raccoonish than ever.

"Did you have your picture taken early in the day? I hope," Jane asked.

Katie was startled. "How'd you know about the pictures? Oh, good. Brownies," she added, giving the lie to Todd's idea of her diet.

"I just know these things," Jane said. Better to let Katie think she'd known all along and had generously let her exercise her own judgment. Since it was too late to do anything about it anyway.

"Did they do anything neat out there today?" Katie asked.

"They might have, but I didn't see it. It's all really tedious and boring to watch."

"Well, I wouldn't know, would I?" Katie said archly. "Since I'm not allowed to set foot in my own backyard."

"I guess you could go out there for a while. As long as you don't go any farther than our yard."

This was more tolerance than Katie really wanted. "Oh, never mind. I'm going to Jenny's. Okay?"

"Back by five," Jane said.

As the door slammed, Jane leaned down and petted Willard. "Why," she asked the big dog, "do I sometimes feel like the desk clerk at a Holiday Inn? And the janitorial service," she added, looking at Todd's backpack on the floor where he'd dropped it.

Willard wagged his tail and drooled happily.

She put together a tuna casserole, crumbling potato chips on the top the way the kids liked it, slid it in the oven, and set the timer—which sometimes worked. She leaned down and listened. Yes, it was making the clicking noise that meant it was going to function. Probably. She got a package of green beans out to thaw, checked that she had what she needed for salad and cornbread. Too much starch for one meal, especially on top of brownies, but they wouldn't die from malnutrition. And as long as tuna wasn't still politically incorrect with Katie, nobody'd complain.

When Jane got outside, people were drifting into the yard and cruising the snack table. The same two extras who'd been telling jokes earlier were still there. "How many writers does it take to change a light bulb?" one asked. "The answer is *NO CHANGES! NO CHANGES!*"

"Move it or lose it!" Butch Kowalski said to them, lunging for a bag of Doritos.

"How did it go?" Jane asked him.

"Perfect! Primo-exacto-perfecto!" Butch said, grinning and popping a chip in his mouth victoriously. "Everything was great. Jake woulda been proud of me. And that Harwell dame, well . . . she was great! I don't usually pay much attention to what the actors are doing, but you couldn't help but watch her."

When George Abington came along a few minutes later, he echoed Butch's sentiments. "You know, I don't mind being acted right off the set for something that good. I hate to say it about Lynette, but that was an Oscar scene. She ought to just retire right this minute so she doesn't screw it up."

Everybody was talking about Lynette's performance. "I'm ashamed to say it, but I got teary on the first take," one wizened extra said. "Ain't cried on a set for thirty years."

"Was she wonderful or what!" another chimed in.

"Someday we can all say we were here today," a breathless girl in a hobble skirt and picture hat said. "Just like the old fogeys say about being on the last scene of *Gone With the Wind*. I'll never forget it."

Cavagnari arrived, looking exhausted. He'd shed his poncho and had sweated through his shirt. He took up the same theme as the extras, but predictably, in a more flamboyant manner.

"We have witnessed a miracle!" he pronounced. "An historic moment in film! Olive! Olive, tell Miss Harwell that all of us salute her!"

Olive Longabach, filling a coffee cup, looked surprised and embarrassed at being singled out, but she still glowed in Lynette's reflected glory. "I will," she mumbled, ducking her head and scurrying off.

"Where is she?" Cavagnari called after her.

"Resting in her dressing room," Olive said, barely slowing down.

"And she deserves to rest. She must be drained! Emotionally spent! Such a performance! Such talent," Cavagnari raved on at Olive's retreating form.

For some reason, his frenzied tone put Jane over the edge. She was suddenly sick of dramatics—fed up with everyone's histrionics, smothered in theatrics. She turned away quickly and went inside. This experience had been interesting, but she was tired of it. She wanted her yard back, her ordinary life back. She wanted to smell her tuna casserole cooking and turn her cats loose and return to normal.

She wanted Jake's murder solved so she could have her weekend with Mel.

——18——

She pulled the curtains on the living room windows so she wouldn't even be tempted to look outside and, on a whim, got out a long-forgotten project. Last year Todd had made a Christmas tree ornament in Cub Scouts that really took her fancy. It was a toy soldier made out of a roundheaded clothespin. She had liked it so well that she'd bought clothespins, assembled all the interesting loose scraps of fabric and trim in her sewing room, and found glue, glitter, acrylic paints, pipe cleaners, and yarn to make more of the dolls. But something had interrupted the project before she got started and she'd put it all away last January. She went searching for the almost-forgotten box, brought it down to the dining room, and laid it all out.

This was the ticket! Something creative and solitary and peaceful that had *nothing* to do with movies or actors. She had promised, months ago, to come up with an idea for something "different" in the way of refrigerator magnets to sell at the next PTA carnival and these little dolls would do fine.

She'd painted faces and made little tutus in different colors for three ballerinas when Katie got home. "Oh, Mom. That's cute," Katie said. "What are you going to use for hair?"

"I don't know. I guess I can't leave them bald. Maybe they could be wearing turbans of the same fabric."

"No, there's something . . ." she closed her eyes for a minute, then dashed off to come back a moment later with a yellow-and-brown sweater with a ripped sleeve. "See? The yarn's all wiggly from being knitted and if you fray it a little, you have hair! Blondes and brunettes."

Jane made another dancer while Katie made and applied hair to the others. Then she disappeared again and returned with a wad of Play-Doh. "What's that for?" Jane asked.

"Boobs."

"Ballerinas don't have boobs."

"This one's going to. She'll be a failure as a ballerina because of them, but will later make a good living modeling underwear for J. C. Penney's ads," Katie said.

Katie got so caught up in the clothespin dolls that she voluntarily helped Jane get dinner on and later cleared so they could go back to them. By eight o'clock that evening, they had a startling array of little people. Soldiers, dancers, a grayish one that Katie maintained was a mailman and Jane said was a Confederate soldier, girls in frilly long dresses, a bride and two matched bridesmaids, and a gypsy with hair from a black sweater Jane had always hated and was happy to sacrifice to the cause.

Jane kept thinking about Shelley's wanting to preserve her daughter in amber at age ten. *This is the evening I want preserved in amber*, Jane thought as they started putting away the fabric and glue and paints.

The doorbell rang and Katie went to let Shelley in. "Jane, I'm glad you're remembering to lock up well. Oh! How darling!" Shelley exclaimed when she saw the dolls.

"They all have life histories. Katie can tell you about them," Jane said. "This one, for example, was a drummer boy from Georgia during the Civil War and was reincarnated as a mailman."

"I'll tell you about the rest of them later, okay? I've got a biology assignment," Katie said. "Good night, Mrs. Nowack."

Shelley sat down looking troubled and waited until Katie was well out of hearing range. "I hate to be the bearer of bad tidings, but have you looked out your back window lately?" she asked quietly. "There are police all over the place again. And an ambulance just pulled away. *Without* the lights flashing. You know what that means."

Jane just stared at her friend for a long moment, then got up and went to the living room window. As she parted the curtains and looked out, she saw Mel coming across the backyard. She and Shelley met him at her kitchen door.

"Mel! What is it?"

"Lynette Harwell is dead. Suicide," he said.

"No!" Shelley exclaimed. "No! Absolutely not. She might be dead, but it wasn't suicide."

"I know it's hard to believe, but—"

"Not hard to believe. Impossible."

"Except that there was no note, it was a classic suicide," Mel explained patiently. "She'd put on her best clothes, done her hair and makeup, took a huge dose of tranquilizers or something, and laid herself out on the couch in her dressing room. She looked like a queen lying in state."

Shelley kept shaking her head. "Not suicide, I tell you. She wouldn't do that. She was the center of the universe. She wouldn't even consider it."

"What happened?" Jane asked. "How did she get away from her keeper long enough for anything to happen to her?"

"It was the keep—er, Miss Longabach, who sent us here. There was some kind of mix-up about the transportation. You see, the stars and the directors have their own limos and drivers to take them back to the hotel downtown where everybody stays. The rest of the out-of-town cast and crew go in vans. Apparently Miss Longabach wasn't allowed to ride with Miss Harwell in the limo—"

"Doesn't that just figure!" Shelley said.

Mel went on, "She went back to wait at the hotel for her. When she didn't come, Miss Longabach assumed she had a dinner engagement and just hadn't mentioned it. After a while, though, she got worried and called Miss Harwell's driver to ask where he'd taken her and with whom. He said he hadn't taken her anyplace, he'd found a note on the front seat of the limo saying she didn't need a ride tonight. That's when Longabach got panicked. She called me. She'd kept my card when I interviewed her earlier. She was embarrassed, said she knew it was just confusion of plans, but to be sure, could I check the set?"

"Why didn't she send somebody from the crew?" Jane asked.

"They don't have cars of their own here, and she said the man in charge of local transportation had gone out for the evening."

"And you found her?" Jane asked.

"In her dressing room in that fancy trailer."

"What about the security people on the set? Don't they leave somebody there all the time?"

"Two men, yes. But they just patrol, looking for intruders or anything out of the ordinary."

"Was her dressing room locked with her inside?" Jane asked.

"No. Unlocked. One of the security men had tested the door and noticed that it was unlocked, but he said it usually was. She either didn't keep any valuables in it or she was too dim to remember to lock up."

"What about the note the driver found in the limo? Did he keep it?"

"He had no reason to. He threw it out in a gas station trash can when he stopped to put some oil in the car and empty the ashtray. He can't remember which station it was, but he's trying to find the receipt. The trash is probably long gone by now."

Shelley had been silent during this exchange. Now she spoke firmly. "Look, Mel. I know you think I'm crazy, but I'd stake my life on the fact that she did *not* commit suicide. The woman was pure ego. But besides that, Jane and I were on the set this afternoon and everybody—even the people who hated her the most—said she'd given the performance of her life today. Nobody could say enough good things about it."

"That's true," Jane said.

Shelley went on, "After years and years of wallowing in mediocrity, she'd finally shined again. Today was, well . . . a springboard to glory. She'd reestablished her talent and celebrity. She had everything to live for and believe me, she'd have wanted to revel in every gratifying second of it. She positively wouldn't have given it up."

Mel looked thoughtful, but said nothing for a long moment. Then, "Jane, do you agree?"

Jane didn't hesitate. "I didn't talk to her much, but if Shelley feels this strongly, I have to agree."

He walked across the kitchen and looked longingly at the coffeemaker. Jane handed him a cup, which he filled and sipped at for a minute. It was the dregs of the pot and must have tasted foul, but he made no sign of distaste, not even a slight flinch, which was a measure of his preoccupation.

Finally he said, "So do I. Agree with Shelley, that is. There's no proof in the world—yet—but my instinct tells me somebody killed her."

——19——

"They have to be connected," Shelley said when Mel had gone back outside to oversee the police examination of the dressing room trailer. "Two people in the same production don't get killed for entirely different reasons by different people."

"How do we know that? I mean it, Shelley. There are more than a hundred people out there every day. Any six of them could be potential mass murderers."

"You're suggesting that six out of a hundred is some kind of national average? You know perfectly well you don't believe that."

"I didn't say I believed it. But it *is* possible."

"But it's more probable that it's one person."

"As far as I'm concerned, they can all kill each other off, so long as they go away. Sorry. I don't mean it. But I do wish they'd go away."

"Jane, you're not thinking very clearly here. They're supposed to be finished tomorrow afternoon and have a wrap party tomorrow night—"

"Surely they'll call *that* off."

"Want to bet?"

"No, I don't think so. But what difference does it make?"

"Jane, Mel could be tied up investigating this thing for months! He can't keep the whole production in town. They're going to scatter like milkweed fluff by Saturday morning."

"Oh. I see what you mean. My weekend with him might be sometime next year."

"Right. And what you said about understanding their motives is dead-on, if you'll excuse the phrase. He looks on all those people as 'foreigners.' Almost 'aliens.' You and I don't understand them a whole lot better, but we're not thrown for quite such a loop as he is."

"I don't know, Shelley. I'd really rather stay out of it, I think. The police can't keep Mel chained to his desk forever."

"Jane . ." Shelley began in a strained voice. "You can't stay out of this."

"I certainly can. I'm not terminally nosy, you know."

"That's not what I meant, exactly."

Jane picked up the now empty coffee carafe and started rinsing it out. "What do you mean?" She put a hearty scoop of coffee into the basket.

Shelley didn't answer right away. "Well—I don't quite know how to say this, but there's something you're overlooking."

"Probably dozens of things, but what did you have in mind?" Jane poured cold water in the coffeemaker and pushed the button to start it brewing before she sat back down across from Shelley at the kitchen table.

"Jane, sooner or later—God, I hate to say this! Sooner or later Mel is going to question everyone about every conversation they heard Lynette Harwell have on this set."

A faint alarm bell went off in the dim recesses of Jane's mind. "Yes?" she said warily.

"And one of her more 'public' conversations was with you and your son about her having had an affair with your husband. Lots of people might have overheard it. You and Mike both went off obviously upset, I assume. All of that is going to be in the record, from interviews with other people."

Jane gulped. "But . . . but . . . ." she sputtered. "I already told him all about it. And about Steve's leaving me. It's got nothing to do with all this."

"Before Lynette was murdered it didn't. But now it's theoretical motive for you to kill her. She did something awful to your child. Told him something you didn't want him to know."

"Mel wouldn't suspect me!"

"Mel-the-guy-you're-dating wouldn't suspect you, but I'm not talking about that person. Detective Mel Van Dyne would have to. At least 'officially.' Now, he'd be hard-pressed to take off a couple extra days to jaunt off with a suspect in an unsolved case."

"But nobody who knows me could think—"

"It's not a question of people who know you. It's the people who don't. Like Mel's boss, whoever that is."

"Oh, hell," Jane murmured. "You're right."

"What's the matter, Mom?" Todd said from the doorway.

Jane smiled automatically. "Nothing at all, honey."

"You got any more of those brownies?"

"I've got another package of mix, if you can wait about twenty minutes," she said. "I'll call you when they're ready."

She flung together a bowl of brownie mix while saying to Shelley, "Okay, let's think sensibly about this. General to the specific, I believe. So, what's a good reason for murdering somebody?"

"There isn't one."

"Not to us. But in theory."

"Okay. Greed comes to mind. Hate. Revenge. Fear. Jealousy. Ambition—"

"Whoa! One at a time, so we can eliminate the most unlikely. Hold it." She spritzed cooking oil on a glass baking dish and hastily dumped the mixture in. Once it was in the oven, she poured them fresh coffee and sat down.

"This is decaf, isn't it?" Shelley asked.

"Of course. If I drank the real stuff this late, I'd be cleaning the oven at four in the morning."

"You can't fool me, Jane. You wouldn't clean an oven if somebody held a gun to your head."

"Maybe not. Okay, I think we can eliminate hate as a motive."

"You do? I'd have put it top on the list. They all seem to hate each other."

"But that's just it. Hate and jealousy both seem natural to most of the people we've gotten to know out there. Cavagnari hates Lynette, so much so that he also hates George Abington for giving her up to him, but he literally works himself into a sweat directing her in a great performance. Lynette hates George Abington, but is convincingly madly in love with him when the camera is rolling. Everybody hates Jake, but speaks well of his particular skills. Likewise everybody seems to hate Lynette, but they fall down praising her when she gives a good performance. It looks to me like hate and jealousy are somehow natural parts of the process. Maybe even necessary parts. An element of emotional 'pumping up' or something."

"Okay, I'll accept all that. Cross off garden-variety hatred. Tentatively. The one I'd eliminate is greed. At least in the case of the principal suspects. They must all have lots of money and I can't imagine how any of them would benefit from either Jake's death or Lynette's."

"Theoretically Butch might have benefited by Jake's death," Jane said.

"Not really. All Jake's props probably belong to his heir now. And that's not likely to be Butch. All Butch has from Jake is the credit that accrued to him from being assistant to a master. That's his whether Jake is alive or dead."

"I don't think for a minute that Butch could have killed anybody, but just for the sake of argument, Jake could have been getting ready to fire him or bad-mouth him. I think we talked about this before. But supposing the same person murdered both of them, what possible reason could Butch have for getting rid of Lynette Harwell?"

"None that I can see," Shelley agreed. "The one

time I saw him speak to her, it was all 'yes, Miss Harwell, no, Miss Harwell, ma'am.' He all but held his hand over his heart and swooned because she'd deigned to speak to him."

"So we can eliminate Butch?"

"I wish you'd stick to one method. We were talking about motives, not suspects. Check your brownies."

Jane turned the pan around so it would cook evenly and sat back down. "Okay, we were talking about greed. We have no idea who Jake's heir might be, unless it's Angela Smith."

"I can't quite feature Angela giving up acting to be a property master. But she might have meant to sell the props to somebody."

"Anybody else who's already a property master would have their own and somebody like Butch, trying to break into the business, wouldn't have any money. Besides, I got the impression that a property master *located* props rather than owning a warehouse full of them."

"You're probably right. We're really hampered by knowing so little about the film business. Let's ignore Jake for the moment. What about Lynette?" Shelley suddenly laughed nervously. "Who would have thought, a week ago, that we'd be sitting here talking about Lynette Harwell as if she were somebody we actually knew!"

"To our sorrow," Jane said glumly. "Well, Lynette was probably loaded. George Abington told me that even bad roles often pay well and she has been working steadily on bad roles for a lot of years."

"Maybe poor old Olive killed her for her money," Shelley offered.

"Are you kidding? Lynette took her for granted. I'll bet she didn't even pay her a decent salary. I can't imagine her making Olive her heir."

Shelley nodded. "That would be like making a carpet your heir, wouldn't it. Lynette seemed to take all that adoration as her just due. What about Lynette's family? Maybe somebody on the set is a long-lost brother."

"George said she came from a rich, social background. Well, that's how she got Olive. She started out as Lynette's nanny. I imagine the rest of the family is well off."

"New motive. Ambition?"

Jane waved this away. "The movie is almost done. How could killing either of them further anybody's career?"

"This movie is almost done. But what about the next one? I wonder if Mel could find out if either of them was contracted for a job after this."

Jane sipped her coffee and thought about this. "Possibly. That makes me think of Jennifer Fortin."

"Me, too."

"Maisie said she was supposed to have wanted this role badly. Maybe Lynette had another good role coming up that she beat Jennifer out of? When Jennifer saw or heard what a great job Lynette did on that last scene, she might have felt she had to clear her out of the way or she'd never have a chance. They look somewhat alike. They're about the same age, and each has one Oscar for a great performance. Maybe the way Jennifer saw it there were certain roles that either of them could play and Lynette was going to get them all from here on."

"That's all perfectly logical, but I don't buy it," Shelley said.

"No, me neither," Jane admitted. "Oh! The brownies!"

When the kids had come and gone, stuffed to the gills with starch and chocolate, Jane said, "I'm still puzzling over the mysterious producers."

"Not again! Jane, why do you keep coming back to that?"

"I don't know. It just seems like it ought to be important. And I have that peculiar feeling that I know something that I don't know I know. Something Katie said when she was making up stories about those clothespin dolls made it come to mind. I wish I could remember what she was talking about at the time."

"Maybe you're right," Shelley said. "There must be a huge amount of money involved in making a movie. And money can be a good motive for murder. As good, or rather, as bad as any other." She glanced at her watch. "Oh! It's after ten! Paul will think I've run away from home."

"Paul's back?"

"Just this evening. Watch me to my door, will you?"

As Shelley opened her kitchen door and waved at Jane, she called out, "Think about those dolls when you go to sleep. Maybe your subconscious will work on it for you."

"My subconscious went on a winter cruise to Bermuda seven years ago and never came home," Jane shouted back.

——20——

Unlike Jake's death, which hardly seemed to make a blip in the progress of the movie, Lynette's got to everybody.

The cast and crew were once again on the set, looking madly busy as the sun rose; this was, after all, the last day and there was much that had to be done. But the mood had changed. Jane could tell that much just from looking out the window at the scene behind her house. The morning was overcast and occasionally the sky spit drizzle, adding to the glum mood. People went about their work with heads down, or glancing over their shoulders furtively when anyone approached behind them.

The press had arrived in ravening hordes. Lynette was well-known; her death was real news. Local papers and television stations sent crews, and all the wire services had gotten the word and also sent people. The police and movie people for once cooperated and banned all the press from the set. A police guard, augmented by private security men and women, was set up to prevent outsiders—including the gawkers—from coming any closer than the street. When Jane had first looked out her front window that morning it was like a reverse parade crowd: instead of mobs standing on the curb looking toward the street, they were standing there trying to see between the houses to the set. It was truly unnerving.

It was more alarming trying to get out to take the kids to school. Jane couldn't have expected any of the car pool drivers to even get on her street. Nor would she have let the kids out of the house to run to their cars if the car pools had made it. She decided to take everybody herself in one trip.

They all got in the car in the garage and as Jane backed the station wagon out she was nearly forced to run over people to get them out of the way. She had the windows rolled up and the doors locked, but they tapped on her windows and shouted questions. Mike, sitting tense and white-faced in the front seat with Jane, gave one reporter a rude gesture which Jane pretended not to notice. Katie and Todd huddled together in the backseat, genuinely frightened.

"They'll all be gone by tomorrow," Jane said, trying to sound calm and reassuring, even though she was deeply shaken. "Would you all like to go from school to your grandmother's this afternoon and spend the night there?"

"Thanks, Mom. Yeah," Katie said, her voice trembling.

"Me, too," Todd said. "I don't like these jerks."

"I'll go home with Scott, okay?" Mike growled.

"All right. I'll pack up stuff for you all. I promise, by tomorrow morning, we won't even know any of this happened."

As they got away from the neighborhood, everybody felt better. On a whim, Jane suggested breakfast at McDonald's since everybody had been too excited and upset to eat at home. The kids thought this was great, especially the idea of getting to be late to school with a note from Mom to explain it.

By the time she finally delivered them to their schools, she felt confident that the trauma of the neighborhood invasion had been smoothed over. But *she* had to go back. For a moment she considered just stopping by the library for a bunch of good books, then checking herself into a nice motel to read and lounge all day, but decided that wasn't the responsible thing to do. Besides, she was just plain curious herself as to how everybody on the set was going to take this new development.

Nobody really bought Lynette's death as a suicide although a few were still trying to romanticize it as such. "She must have known she could never do better than yesterday," Jane overheard somebody saying. "She wanted to go out in a blaze of glory, I think."

But most of the cast and crew were uneasy, obviously feeling threatened that a murderer was among them. It was odd, Jane thought, that Jake's death, which was so unmistakably a murder, hadn't made them nervous, but Lynette's demise, which might (in spite of Shelley's and Mel's instincts) have been suicide, frightened them all. Jane supposed it was because in a strange way suicide *is* scarier than murder. We can lock ourselves in our houses and hide from killers, but there's nowhere to hide from ourselves.

Shelley was already outside and had been eavesdropping. "What's up now?" Jane asked her in a hushed tone.

"Olive arrived a while ago, looking like a corpse herself, poor old thing. I guess she came to pick up Lynette's things. The rumor is that there was a ring in Lynette's dressing room that wasn't hers."

"Whose was it?"

"The gossip mill says it was Angela's."

"Interesting. I wonder how Angela explains that."

"Apparently she can't. The word is that she says she kept it in her purse and didn't even realize it was missing until the police asked her to identify it."

"Not very likely," Jane said. "Even if it was in her purse and just fell out, it fell out in Lynette's dressing room and that's very damning. Angela is connected to Jake, either as his girlfriend or his niece, but did she have any previous connection with Lynette?"

"I can't find anybody who knows of any," Shelley said.

Jane glanced around, noticing that the weather had cleared and was promising to turn into a very nice day for their final scenes. Suddenly she saw somebody who made her nearly scream. She damped it down to a squeak. "My God! I thought that was Lynette!"

Shelley looked where Jane pointed. Jennifer Fortin was in conversation with Roberto Cavagnari. She was dressed in the same costume Lynette had worn the day before and had her hair fixed in the same style. She looked astonishingly like the dead actress.

"How creepy!" Shelley exclaimed. She left Jane gaping and went to chat for a minute with some extras standing around the coffee urn. When she came back, she said, "They had some long shots to do of Lynette and George. Jennifer is filling in. Didn't they do that in Jean Harlow's last movie?"

"Oh, yes. I remember seeing the scenes that were supposed to be Harlow at a racetrack or something. All three-quarter shots of the back of her head. But it was somebody else because Harlow had died. I see how it's necessary, but it's still nasty."

Jane learned a little more about it when she went to fix herself a cup of coffee. The producers' representative was using the phone as she stood a few feet away. He punched in a long set of numbers. *So it's long-distance*, Jane thought to herself.

"Yes, hello. Is V. J. there?" he asked. "Yes, Claude here. Just checking in. It's a zoo, as you could guess. No, Roberto says he can finish by four as long as the security people keep the press out of his hair. They're getting ready for the long shots of scene nineteen."

He paused, listening. "No, Roberto must have called Fortin. She's doing them. Didn't even ask for credits. Just scale. My guess is she's sucking up to Cavagnari. Oh, sure I did. I don't let anybody near here without a signed contract. Not to worry."

Jane got very busy picking over the donuts as if which one to choose were a life-and-death decision. Not that she needed a donut, but she wanted a reason to stay in place.

"Listen, Veronica, everything's really all right, given the mess," the young man was going on. "We didn't need Harwell today except for the long shots. And the kid doing the props is fine. Don't worry about the press. I'm just sorry we're getting all this attention now instead of closer to the release date. Now, I've got a problem with George's home ticket. It's for the wrong day. Could you get it straightened out at your end? Uh-oh, a reporter's got hold of Olive. Gotta go!"

In fact, several reporters had gotten through the security cordon and had hold of Olive. Or perhaps she had latched onto them. Jane's heart ached for the older woman, who looked pale and ill. Her eyes were red and her face blotched and she was hanging onto an assortment of canvas bags and dresses on hangers, which made her look like a refugee fleeing a disaster with all her worldly goods.

But she seemed to have a grip on herself in spite of it all. At least for the moment. "I will not comment on Miss Harwell's death," she was saying to a gathering crowd. The producers' nerd was trying to shoo them away, but to no avail. "But I will talk about her life and her work. She was the finest actress of the century and when the world sees the work she did on this, her last film, she will take her rightful place in the history of the film industry."

"How did she die?"

"Who are you?"

"Where's she being buried?"

The questions came fast, overlapping each other.

"This film represents the finest achievement of her career," Olive went on, as if giving a rehearsed speech. Maybe it was, Jane thought. "This role and her remarkable performance will be a tribute, an eternal tribute, to a fine actress."

"That's enough, boys!" George Abington had appeared, grabbed Olive's arm, and pushed her through the crowd, flinging reporters aside like bowling pins. "Olive," he said firmly. "Drop all that stuff. There are people to carry it for you. Just come over here and have some tea. Those people won't bother you again."

"Let me fix you some tea, Miss Longabach," Jane said. "Do you take sugar?"

"Lemon and sugar. Yes, please," Olive said, her voice starting to crack. Jane wondered for a second if she and George were the only people in the world who'd ever offered to do anything *for* Olive. George had scattered the last of the reporters by the time Jane got to the old woman with a hot cup of tea and a paper plate with a donut.

"I'm very sorry about your—about Miss Harwell, Miss Longabach," Jane said.

"Thank you, dear. It's terrible . . . just terrible. I feel so awful that I wasn't with her . . ."

"Now, now. Don't think about that. Would you like for me to keep her things in my house until somebody can pick them up?"

George was still standing guard over her. "Don't bother, Jane. I've already arranged to have them sent back to the hotel. Olive, you should stay here today. I don't want you back there by yourself. Roberto may need you, too. And there's a wrap party tonight, you know," he went on. "You must come."

"Oh, no. I couldn't."

"But you must come in Lynette's place," George insisted. "You know she'd want you here, and so will the cast and crew. If we can't have her, we must have you. Very few of these people will be able to come to the funeral, but they'll want to say their good-byes through you."

It was a gracious gesture, beautifully done, Jane thought. George Abington might consider himself a plumber of an actor, but he was a nice man. He'd sensed that Olive Longabach would have been miserable and lonely this evening by herself, but had appealed to her psychotically overdeveloped sense of duty to Lynette to get her out.

"Well, if I must—"

Maisie had joined them, checking on Olive's well-being and Jane felt free to wander off. She spotted the production assistant who always found her when it was time to let Willard out and waved that she understood the message.

As she brought him outside, Shelley was just putting her little orange poodle Frenchie into his smaller dog run. "Shelley, did you ever know anybody named Veronica?" Jane asked.

Shelley unsnapped Frenchie's collar, closed the gate, and leaned on it. "I don't think so. Oh, yes. A girl in my grade school."

"And what did you call her?"

"Call her? Ronnie, I think. Why on earth do you ask?"

"Because I have a sneaking suspicion I know who the mysterious producers are."

——21——

"What did you say your wife's name was?" Jane asked George Abington a few minutes later.

She and Shelley had tracked him down in his dressing room, which was the other half of the same trailer that housed Lynette's space. It was very nice, but quite cramped and impersonal. There was a couch/sofa, a table big enough to eat or do paperwork or play cards with one friend, an open closet, a counter beneath a well-lighted mirror, a couple of chairs, and visible through another door, a train compartment–style bathroom.

George was sitting at the small table and had apparently been studying his script when the brads holding it together had come apart. He fussed with the pages, trying to get the holes lined up. "My ex-wife, you mean? Mrs. Johnson," he said. "Why do you ask?"

"Ronnie, I think you called her," Jane persisted.

"Yes. Hell! Where did that other thing go?" He leaned down and looked at the carpet for the other brad.

"George, is your ex-wife one of the producers of this movie?"

He finally gave up pretending interest in the reassembly of the script and smiled. "You're clever, Jane. Yes. She is."

"And are you another?"

He nodded.

"And who else?"

"Who do *you* think?" he shot back, grinning.

"Lynette Harwell."

"Bingo. How in the world did you figure it out? Am I such a poor actor that I gave it away or did Lynette blab?"

"Nobody blabbed. I just heard your rep on the phone, addressing the person he was speaking to as Veronica. And I remembered you calling your wife Ronnie. I also remembered you saying you'd made good money doing so many roles and I figured Lynette probably had, too."

"Come on, Jane. There are a lot of Veronicas in the world and a lot of actors who are fairly well off."

"But there aren't a lot of producers who would risk putting a ton of money into a movie starring Lynette Harwell—except Lynette herself. She hadn't made a decent movie for ten years and was considered a jinx besides."

George nodded at the logic of this.

"I asked myself, why would you agree to work with her, given your personal history, unless you had money in it, too? And you did say your wife was wealthy and had kept in touch with the business, but not as an actress. You also mentioned how good she was with contractual things in the movie business. So instead of having absent producers, you had two of the three on the set, right in the middle of things, and a third handling the money from a safe distance."

"You'd make a good detective."

Jane hoped he'd never repeat this remark in front of Mel, who could be counted on to take umbrage at such an assessment of her leanings.

"How did this all happen?" Shelley asked.

George leaned back and laced his fingers together over his stomach. "Ronnie and I read the book years ago. While we were still married. I was starting to do pretty well by then and we bought the film option from the author. Then Lynette came along and our marriage went to pot. But we kept joint ownership of the film rights and kept renewing the option because we knew it would pay off someday. Then about two years ago Olive Longabach happened on the book and saw it as a good film opportunity for Lynette. She contacted the publisher and learned who owned the rights. Lynette contacted Ronnie, who suggested that instead of getting into a bidding war for the option renewal, the three of us get together and produce it instead."

"So, let me see if I follow this. You and your ex-wife agreed to bring in your other ex-wife, who took you away from the first wife, and hire the man who broke up your second marriage to direct it?" Shelley asked, shell-shocked.

George shrugged and grinned. "What can I say? Hollywood. Wonderful, weird place. It was the right property for everybody. I got a good role, Lynette got a great one. If it does as well as we think it will, the cable rights alone will keep us all in luxury for a good long time. Even the original author's heirs are thrilled. They've gotten a terrific paperback reprint offer and the old book will have a whole new life."

Shelley was still shaking her head in wonder.

A production assistant stuck her head in the door. "Mr. Abington, we need you for a minute to get a light reading."

"Be right back. See if you can't get that damned script put back together for me, would you?" he said as he left.

Jane and Shelley sat and stared at each other for a minute. "Jane, I'm amazed. That was really clever of you."

"Not as much as it sounds like. It was what was bothering me last night. I was almost asleep when I remembered another one of Katie's doll stories. She said her doll had been a secretary who had been so much more beautiful than the others that they hated her, but she got them back by marrying the head of the corporation and firing them all. It just seemed like a possibility somehow—that the producers were staying undercover because they were too well acquainted with somebody here, but I didn't really know how until I heard that guy on the phone this morning."

"See? You do have a resident subconscious. It didn't really move to Bermuda." Shelley picked up the script and knocked it briskly on a table to get the pages realigned.

"Just in for a fleeting visit, I'm afraid. But I kept thinking the producers were secretly trying to *get back* at somebody and that didn't make sense. Why risk a huge amount of money to get even with someone. Instead, they were *promoting* somebody. Two of themselves."

"Well, now we know what Jake was blackmailing Lynette about," Shelley said. She'd found the missing brad and threaded it through the holes in the script.

"Probably so. But how did he know?"

Shelley shook her head. "I don't suppose we'll ever find out. He'd been around the business a long time, though, and knew everybody. Maybe he heard the front guy calling George's wife and put it together, too."

"But that would only lead him to George. Not Lynette."

"It led *you* to Lynette."

"You're right. But Shelley, I still don't see how it helps us. I hate to admit that after my 'brilliant' deduction. What if Jake was blackmailing her about being a producer? He must have known the same about George, and he tried something entirely different on him and it was easier to figure out George's connection than Lynette's. Anyway, even if it helped explain why Jake was killed, it doesn't help with Lynette's death. I can't quite see her killing Jake, then doing away with herself out of remorse. She probably had no concept of remorse."

"Unless—"

"Unless?" Jane asked.

Shelley lowered her voice. "Unless it was George trying to keep it all a secret. *And now the two of us know.*"

"Oh—!"

Shelley set the script down as if it were a bomb and they both rose and quickly headed for the door. But George was standing just outside.

"Where are you going, ladies?"

Did he sound menacing or was it Jane's imagination going into overdrive?

"No, no. We don't want to disturb you anymore."

"I haven't got a thing to do for another hour." He came in the door, sweeping them before him.

"Look, George—Mr. Abington, we're going to have to tell the police what we know. In fact—" Jane started to say they already had, but was cut off.

"I don't think they'll be too surprised."

"Why?"

"Because I told them last night when they were collecting alibis."

"You told them already?"

"Of course. It wasn't *that* deep cover a secret. In fact, we had a press release written up to present at the wrap party tonight. There was a copy in Lynette's dressing room. The police found it and asked me about it."

Jane didn't know whether to be relieved or angry. She settled on angry. "Then why the hell was it a secret to begin with!" she snapped.

"Why, for Cavagnari's sake, of course," he said, as if this should have been obvious to an especially backward four-year-old.

Seeing their blank expressions, he explained patiently. "Ladies, directors are a touchy lot. They will work for producers, any producers. The producers can be mob bosses or survivalists, as long as they have the money to put up. But directors hate working for actors. They consider us below them in the food chain and we damned well better stay there. Roberto didn't mind taking orders from an orthodontist's wife from Encino. Just as long as he didn't know two of his actors were also giving the orders. But as of tonight, Roberto's main work is done. In a few hours, it won't matter. He's still got to oversee the cutting, but we won't be underfoot. Well, even if Lynette hadn't died, I mean."

"Okay, George. So you're saying Jake wouldn't have been trying to blackmail Lynette over this?" Shelley asked. She sounded as irritable as Jane was feeling.

"Oh, he might have been trying. But Lynette probably wouldn't have much cared. It all happened so close to the end of filming anyhow."

"But her most important scene was yesterday. She wouldn't have wanted the director to know before that, would she?"

George thought a moment. "I don't think it would have mattered. Lynette had that scene down cold. She didn't need Roberto to tell her how to do it."

"I don't get it," Shelley said. "She seemed so vain and stupid. And yet, you're saying she created a marvelous performance out of that empty head? And before that, helped put together the financing for the whole deal?"

"I guess she was sort of an idiot savant," George said. "Dumb as a chicken about most things and brilliant in a very few."

"Who killed her?" Jane asked, hoping to surprise valuable information out of George.

"No idea," he said cheerfully. "Not my problem, thank God."

—— 22 ——

"Can we believe him?" Shelley asked as the two walked back to their "home base" in Jane's yard.

"About what?"

"Everything. Anything."

"I think I probably do. We don't have much choice. Besides—" Jane explained to Shelley about George's being so nice to poor old Olive a little while earlier. "It's entirely possible that he may know more than he's telling us. He may even be lying about what he *is* telling us, but I'm absolutely certain the man isn't a killer. I think his instincts are basically kindly."

As they came through the gap in the scenery, they met up with Mel. "There you two are. I've been looking for you. I've got to get away from here for ten minutes. Want to go someplace for coffee?"

"Sure. I'll drive," Jane said. "You're probably parked fourteen miles away anyhow and I'd like to get another shot at running over a reporter. It's something I think I could be good at with a little practice."

"I've got to run home for a minute first," Shelley said. "I'll meet you in your garage."

"Jane, I'm really sorry," Mel said, taking her arm possessively as they headed for her house. "About this weekend, I mean."

Jane glanced at her watch. "So am I. Right now we'd have been heading for the airport."

"Another time. As soon as this is sorted out."

"Are you getting close to solving the murders?"

"I'll tell you all about it when we get away from here."

They went in through the kitchen door and back out to the garage from the inside entrance. They sat in the car in the dark garage for a minute. Mel kissed her long and hard, then Jane sighed and pushed the garage door opener. Shelley was waiting outside, smiling as if she'd guessed what caused the delay.

They went to a family restaurant a few blocks away, which was nearly deserted. The breakfast crowd had gone and the lunchers hadn't arrived yet. Mel got them a booth in the far corner and ordered coffee all around.

"So?" Jane said when the waitress had come and gone. She hadn't much liked the hungry looks the young woman had given Mel. Nor had she been pleased with the fact that the waitress was dressed in a very flattering uniform while Jane herself was in gray sweats.

"So, I guess you heard about Angela's ring being in Harwell's dressing room."

"Just gossip. Is it true?"

He nodded. "She claimed at first that she'd never been in there, but we had questioned somebody who saw her knocking at the door the first day of shooting.

Then she admitted she'd been lying before and that she had gone in. It was the day before Harwell died and Angela could well have claimed that's when she lost the ring, but she didn't."

"I doubt that would really have worked," Jane said. "I'll bet Olive knows every inch of that trailer."

"Yes, and the ring was in plain sight on the makeup counter, but it's the one thing that makes me tend to believe Angela—the fact that she had a legitimate excuse for the ring being there, but kept denying that it could have been."

"What do you mean?" Shelley asked.

"She claims it was in her purse and she didn't have her purse with her when she visited Harwell."

"Why was she there at all?" Jane asked.

"To have a fight with Harwell. No, that's not true. She claims she went in just to ask Harwell nicely if she would use her influence to get her the part the chicken pox girl had left vacant. She also says she wanted to apologize for Jake's attempt to blackmail her. That's when the feathers started flying."

"Why?"

"Harwell took offense. Said nobody had ever tried to blackmail her and they'd better not try. Angela says—and this, mind you, is all just her word—that Harwell got the mistaken impression that Angela herself had come to practice a little extortion. The more Angela tried to explain, the madder Harwell got. Angela says she was being so stupid and dramatic that she wanted to shake her. Angela finally said something sharp and nasty, she claims she doesn't remember just what it was, but I don't believe that. Anyway, Harwell tried to slap her, and Angela ducked out."

"That's all?"

"That's all she says. It's possible that she went away and got madder and madder about it. Figured Harwell would bad-mouth her in the business, then went back the next afternoon and poisoned her tea."

"Is that what happened? Poison?"

"Not exactly. Sleeping pills. A huge dose. The pathologist says he's got a lot more tests to run, but he's pretty sure that was the cause."

"Where'd the sleeping pills come from?" Jane asked.

"They were Harwell's. Legitimate prescription. Refilled the day before. The cup was still in the trailer. Preliminary tests showed traces in the bottom."

"Anything else? Any injuries? Sign of struggle?"

Mel shook his head. "Nothing immediately obvious. It looks like a nice, quiet suicide. The tea must have tasted awful. She couldn't have drunk it accidentally without noticing something strange. And I guess I told you, she was laid out as if she were ready to be popped right into a coffin. Fancy dress. Hair and makeup perfect. Hands neatly crossed."

"Are you wavering about it being suicide?" Shelley asked.

"Not at all. Just telling you the impression it's giving everybody else."

They were quiet for a moment while the waitress refilled their cups. Jane wondered again why she hadn't just put on a skirt and blouse this morning instead of the baggy outfit she'd chosen without any thought.

"Anything else of significance in the dressing room?" Jane asked. "Oh! We forgot to ask you. Did you really find a press release saying who the producers were?"

"Yes. How did you know about that?"

"George Abington told us."

"I wish you two wouldn't meddle in this. I appreciate having someone to talk to about cases, but it scares the stuffing out of me when you two start doing your 'junior detective' stuff."

Shelley ignored the warning. "Do you think there's a connection? Between the murders and the secret about the producers, I mean."

"There might be, but I'm damned if I can see what it is. I'll admit, though, that I'm beginning to wonder if the blackmail had anything at all to do with either murder."

"Why is that?" Jane asked.

"Well, think about it," Mel said, leaning forward. "It was over something so trivial. Jake just wanted Angela to get a little part. I'll grant you, I don't know much about the movie business, but that's still a stupid reason. It wasn't a big part. I've studied the script. It was a few lines that were only designed to give the main character someone to talk to. The character part didn't even have a name. It was just 'farm girl,' and she said things like, 'What do you mean?' so that Harwell's character could go off into a monologue. I can see how Angela would have liked to have the part, but if she'd gotten it and done the greatest acting in history, it wouldn't have done her much good. I'm finding it hard to believe that two people could have met their deaths because of something that insignificant."

"Maybe Jake was really blackmailing them about something else entirely," Shelley suggested.

"Or maybe it had nothing to do with the blackmail," Mel repeated. "It doesn't make sense."

"But it does, in a way," Jane said. "I can't claim to have known Jake very well, but from what everybody's said, it would have been like him to go overboard and use a sledgehammer to kill a gnat. Everybody says he was great with objects and lousy with people. He apparently had no sense of proportion in relationships. I can imagine him deciding there was something he wanted and just using the first tool at hand, which was blackmail, instead of something appropriate, like simply asking that Angela be given consideration for the part."

Mel shrugged. "I guess there are people like that. I'm glad I don't know any of them personally."

The waitress drifted by again, giving Mel a melting smile which Jane was extremely glad to see that he didn't return or even acknowledge.

"There's something else—" he said. "There was a religious medallion on the sink in the bathroom."

"Not Lynette's?"

"Nope."

"Whose?" Jane asked.

"Butch Kowalski's, I'm afraid."

Jane shivered. "Certainly not?"

"It had his name engraved on the back. It didn't take a lot of 'detecting' to figure it out."

"You've talked to him about it?" Shelley asked.

Mel nodded. "He just says he doesn't know how it got there. He wore it on a chain around his neck, but the chain broke a couple days ago and he stuffed it in his pocket. He claims that he took it out at some point to see if he could fix the chain, but can't remember where he put it next."

"And you think that sounds fishy?" Jane asked.

Mel laughed. "I don't think 'fishy' is the word I'd have used, but it is pretty thin."

"It could be the truth," Jane said.

"Sure it could. But is it?" Mel replied.

"Did anybody see him around the dressing room trailer at the relevant time?" Shelley asked. "What *is* the relevant time anyway?"

"Sometime after five and before nine. The pathology people wouldn't give me anything better than that until they've done all their magic. But Olive saw her at five. Harwell asked her to take a dress that needed mending to wardrobe, and not to come back because she was going to rest for an hour. Olive took the five-thirty van without seeing her again."

"And do you know where Angela and Butch were during that time?"

"We know where they say they were. Angela was three different places; makeup, wardrobe, and at craft services making a phone call to a dry cleaners who'd lost something of hers. The dry cleaners confirm the call. Various people saw her at all three places, but it would have taken only a few minutes to slip into the trailer along the way and dump the contents of the capsules into Harwell's tea."

"But wouldn't Harwell have thought that was a little odd? Somebody ducking in her trailer and messing around with her stuff?" Jane asked.

"Not if she was taking a nap like she told Olive," Shelley said.

"Or if she'd left the trailer for a minute," Mel added.

"But this foul-tasting tea would have been cold by that time."

"Longabach said she usually drank it lukewarm," Mel said. "That it hurt her teeth if it was hot."

"What about Butch? Where was he after five?" Jane asked.

"Same story. All over the place. Putting away props. Nobody was with him the whole time. He and the assistant went back and forth from the set to the prop trailer. Passed each other a couple times, but the same time element applies to him. He had his own car since he's local. He says he left the set at six. No real alibi."

"But Mel, I don't *want* Butch to be the murderer," Jane said.

"I'm sorry, but that's not exactly a consideration," Mel answered. "Since you two have been snooping, you might tell me what, if anything, you've learned. What are people talking about this morning?"

"About Lynette's death, mainly," Shelley said. "I guess you'll be glad to hear that most of the crew doesn't believe it was suicide either."

"Everybody's relieved that it didn't happen before the filming finished, naturally," Jane added. "More than relieved. They seem to be stuck in a groove about how ironic and fitting it was that she managed to give the performance of her life only hours before she died. The 'out in a blaze of glory' theme is getting a lot of play."

"Not very helpful." Mel glanced at his watch. "I've got to get back."

"What are you going to do next?" Shelley asked.

"God knows," he said glumly.

——23——

When Jane got home the cats were being so pathetic about their long incarceration that she decided to let them outside. So what if they wandered through a scene? It would just add a touch of realism, she decided.

She opened the kitchen door and Max streaked out like a lightning bolt, got about ten feet before he noticed the crowd, then whirled and streaked back. "You thought they'd gone?" she asked him. "Or had your little kitty brain forgotten that they were ever here? I wish I could forget this." She held the door open patiently while he made a second, more cautious exit with Meow creeping along behind him. They stretched their necks, taking in the unfamiliar smells for a bit before they headed for the foundation plantings and disappeared.

Butch Kowalski had been watching this performance and approached her. "Poor things," he said, smiling as Max reemerged briefly to arch his back for a pet. "I'll bet you'll all be glad to have your yard back to yourselves."

"It's not so much the yard as far as they're concerned. It's the field. That's their hunting ground.

They think they're wild cats when they're prowling out there."

"No cat food bushes, though. Well, it'll be trampled for a while, but all the equipment will be gone by tomorrow night. Some of it will be moved out by tonight. Are you coming to the wrap party?"

"Am I invited?" Jane asked to avoid giving a direct answer. The last thing in the world she wanted to do was draw out her relationship with most of these people. No, that wasn't fair, she chided herself. Some of them were quite likable. Butch, for one.

"Sure you're invited," Butch said. "I wish you'd come. It would be nice to have at least one friendly face there."

"What do you mean by that?"

"Come on. You've heard the gossip about me, haven't you? Everybody's treating me like Jack the Ripper. Sure, it was my boss who died, but I don't get anything out of it. I'd be stupid to off Jake. He was my paycheck. Besides—I really kinda liked the guy."

"You did?"

"I know. He was a real jerk about a lot of things. But he treated me good enough. Took me on when I didn't know shit about the business, and took a lot of time teaching me stuff. Everything I know was because of him. If it wasn't for him, I'd still be driving a delivery van with no damned future at all." His face was getting red.

"What's your future now, Butch?"

"I guess I gotta set out on my own. And it's not gonna be easy. I talked to Roberto—before Miss Harwell died—and he said he'd put me in touch with a guy who does a lot of commercials around here. I'm gonna have to start pretty well down the ladder on my own. No movies, but I might get commercial jobs and work back up to movies. Don't you see? If Jake was still alive, I could have gotten a lot more credits and contacts with the big-time people before I went on my own. I wouldn't kill him off. Mrs. Kowalski didn't raise no stupid kids."

"What about your medallion?" Jane decided to ask since Butch was being so frank.

He didn't seem surprised that she knew about the medallion. He assumed that everybody on the set knew about it, which was probably true. "I don't know! I just can't figure that. I had it in my pocket 'cause the chain busted. I got a free minute somewhere along the line, and I remember getting it out to see if I could fix it, but then somebody needed me for something and I guess I just put it down. I just can't remember. It wasn't important at the time."

"Was this yesterday?"

"I think so. I got the feeling it was in the morning sometime, but like I say, it wasn't that important and I'm not sure."

"And you were never in Miss Harwell's dressing room?"

"Are you kidding? A slob like me? Hanging around the likes of her?"

"Do you think somebody put it there on purpose to implicate you?"

"I dunno. Maybe. Or maybe she found it wherever I left it and just set it out meaning to ask whose it was and forgot. Or somebody else picked it up and left it there by accident. The police asked me all this and seemed real pissed that I didn't have any good ideas about it."

"Butch, I'm really sorry about this. It's not fair to you."

"Yeah, but Jake woulda said, 'You ain't got Fair in your contract.' He had a lot of stuff like that he said. I'm really gonna miss him. That's why it makes me so mad, people acting like I killed him. And then thinking I mighta done anything bad to Miss Harwell—that's crazy! Did you watch that scene yesterday?"

"Only from a distance."

"Well, let me tell you, she was—" he groped around, trying to come up with the right word, and finally produced one that surprised Jane. "Stunning. She was stunning."

"Let's sit down a minute, Butch. You haven't got a cigarette on you, have you? I left mine inside."

"God, no. I had to give up smoking when I started working for Jake."

"Oh, yeah. There's no worse crusader than an ex-smoker, is there?"

"What do you mean? Jake never smoked."

"Oh? I thought he did—" something clicked in the back of Jane's brain.

"Naw, his mom died of lung cancer when he was a kid. He never smoked and never let anybody who worked for him smoke either."

"But why did I think—?"

"*Quiet on the set!*" someone behind Jane bellowed.

At the same moment, the intern came plunging through between the pieces of scenery and said, "Butch—"

"Rolling," the bullhorn announced.

The set was utterly silent. The intern froze in place and gestured to Butch. Butch responded with a quick movement of his fingers.

Jane put a hand over her mouth to keep from exclaiming. Hand signals! Signing! That's why she thought Jake was an ex-smoker. The way his hand kept fidgeting at lunch. But it wasn't nerves. It was signing! In complete silence, he'd been "talking" to someone.

The next couple of minutes seemed to last for hours. Jane's mind lurched and wheeled, circling memories, picking some, rejecting others, fitting pieces together, trying to make pieces fit that refused to.

"Cut!"

Without another word to Butch, Jane leaped out of her lawn chair and sprinted to where she thought she'd seen Shelley standing a few minutes before. But Shelley was gone. "Maisie!" Jane said, spotting a familiar face. "Have you seen Shelley?"

"I think she's talking to somebody over by the props truck."

Jane headed that way and met Shelley coming back. "Quick! We have to find Mel and talk to him. I just realized something!"

"He's at the dressing room trailer."

He was interviewing someone and they had to wait a few minutes. "What is this?" Shelley asked in a whisper.

"Not here," Jane said. "Inside. Privately."

An electrician emerged from the trailer and Jane darted inside. "Mel, I've got to talk to you. At my house where nobody else can hear us."

She all but dragged him across the field.

Once they were all inside and well away from anyone who might overhear, Jane explained. "I don't know if anybody mentioned this to you, Mel, but Jake made his workers all learn to sign."

"You hauled me in here to tell me *that*?"

"Yes. It's important. He was doing it at that lunch the day he was killed. I noticed, but then I forgot about it. It was after he'd finished eating and he kept fidgeting his fingers, as if he were antsy for a cigarette to handle. I just figured he was a recently reformed smoker and didn't give it any more thought. But you see? He was giving someone a message!"

Mel wasn't convinced. "What if he was? We'll never know what it was. I don't see how it helps us—"

Jane had suddenly stepped back, her eyes wide! "But we might—! The tape!"

"Jane, have you gone over the edge," Shelley said. "What are you babbling about? What tape?"

"Somebody was taping the lunch! Roberto found out about it and had a fit. He ripped the tape out of the camcorder and gave it to me to throw away!"

"What did you do with it?" Mel asked, getting interested.

"I have no idea! Oh, *hell*! What did I do with it?"

"Don't get hysterical," Mel said sharply. "Just calm down and think it through. He handed you the tape and—?"

"He didn't really hand it to me, he sort of threw it at me. And I—I stuffed it into the big front pocket of the sweatshirt I was wearing. Then—then Lynette started that horrible story about her and Steve! I just don't know! Maybe I dropped it."

She closed her eyes, trying to bring back the terrible memory of the next few minutes. "I came inside. Upstairs. I tried to talk to Mike, but he was mad and stomped out. I went in my room—"

She opened her eyes again and without a word turned and ran upstairs. A few seconds later, she came running back down with the tape cassette held high. "I kicked it under the bed. Shelley, turn on the television."

She shoved the tape into the maw of the VCR. The three of them leaned forward, nearly ear to ear, watching as the luncheon replayed. It seemed endless. People came and went, passed the camera, blotting out the people at the table momentarily. Roberto's endless story went on and on.

"Fast forward the thing," Mel ordered. "No. Stop! There."

The photographer had a good long shot of the table. Jake's hand was clearly visible.

"That's signing, all right," Mel said. "Hold it, I've got to call the office." He returned a minute later. "One of the secretaries signs. She's on her way over. You haven't cleaned your kitchen real well lately, have you?"

Jane looked at him with surprise. "Mel, I've got dust bunnies so old they're collecting social security. Of *course* I haven't cleaned my kitchen 'real well' lately. Why?"

"Because this tape may explain who was in your house and why."

"I don't get—"

"They were looking for this tape, Jane. Somebody knew what Jake had said and didn't want a record of it. They must have left fingerprints when they wrecked the place hunting."

"Or maybe Jake himself wanted it," Shelley said.

"Whoever it was, I'm going to have to fingerprint the kitchen and then start fingerprinting everybody out there. We hadn't done that because there weren't prints on the knife to compare to and the only ones on the tea mug were Harwell's and Longabach's, which were supposed to be on it. It's going to be a long afternoon, ladies. And we don't yet know if this damned tape will be any help at all."

──24──

They ran the tape several times. The secretary Mel had summoned translated for them.

"He's talking to Lynette, of course," Jane said. "They go way back together and he must have known she had a brother who was deaf and assumed she'd understand the signing. It certainly explains Butch's medallion, doesn't it?"

"It might," Mel said. "But we can't be sure. It's not proof. Conjecture won't get me anyplace except pointed in the right direction."

"But you can find out whether what he was saying is true, can't you? Subpoena records—?" Jane asked.

Mel nodded. "But even then—maybe nobody cared that much if it was known."

"It doesn't look to me as if she's registering any acknowledgment of what he's saying," Shelley said.

"She was an actress. Putting expression in her face was her life's work. Maybe she's just as good at keeping it out," Jane replied.

"Maybe she didn't understand," Shelley said quietly. "Would someone that self-absorbed bother to learn signing just so she could talk to her little brother? He probably lip-read, too."

Jane looked at her. "I think you're probably right, Shelley. So, if she didn't get it, who did?"

"It could be anybody at or around that table," Shelley said. "What do we know about them? Lots of people can sign well enough to have gotten the gist of it. I'll bet you Katie knows the signing alphabet. There was quite a fad with the girls at school last year to learn it. They thought it was fun. Like a secret code."

Mel said, "I've got my men asking around if any of the others at that table have anyone in their family with a hearing problem. But it still doesn't *prove* anything. It's possible that this has nothing to do with the murders. And even if it does, it's only a reason to kill Jake—and certainly not Lynette."

"I know," Jane said sadly.

"Jane, I appreciate your help. Really. It's not your fault this wasn't as useful as we'd all hoped."

"Mel, just rerun it one more time. I'm sure there's something there that will help."

He obligingly rewound the tape and played it again. "Okay, who's able to see what he's doing?" Jane asked. "George is on his left. He might be able to see Jake's right hand. And Lynette is directly across from him acting like she doesn't notice either him or Olive standing behind her like a Secret Service agent. You can just see Butch at the edge of the frame, sitting on a folding chair with his lunch in his lap. But his face is out of the picture most of the time. We can't see what he's looking at."

"Cavagnari keeps looking Jake's way," Shelley said.

"Right, maybe because Jake's the only one who appears to be listening to him. Or maybe because he's 'listening' to Jake," Jane said.

"Angela and the intern are at the end of the table," Shelley went on. "It's hard to tell from this angle if they could see his right hand, what with all the drinking glasses that might have been in their line of sight."

"Angela must know signing," Jane said. "She was Jake's niece and it was one of his professional gimmicks. The intern had to learn it to work with him."

"The problem is, we have no way of knowing who else was just out of camera range," Shelley said.

"No, the problem is that this gives Lynette a very slight, possible reason to have killed Jake, but nobody a reason to have killed Lynette," Mel said harshly. "I'm sorry, but it's really no help at all. Charlene, thanks for coming over so quickly," he added to the secretary.

She was a plump, pretty woman of about thirty. She sighed and picked up her purse and sweater. "I'm sorry I wasn't able to help more. This is such a sad, sad thing, Lynette Harwell dying like that. I've sort of followed her career. Seen a couple of really bad movies just because she was in them and I kept hoping she'd be terrific again someday."

"Well, she was terrific yesterday," Jane said. "Shelley and I watched from a distance and really couldn't hear much, but everybody on the set said she gave her best performance ever."

"Well, at least she went out in style then," Charlene said. "Not all of us can lay claim to that much."

"I'm afraid that's true," Shelley said.

"And to think she was a—" Charlene stopped. "Well, it doesn't matter now, does it? She's got at least two really outstanding performances that will outlast her. Her family and friends and all her many fans will have to find a way to take comfort from that, I suppose. Mel, I've got some papers in the car for you. If you want to walk with me—"

They headed out through the kitchen, where two men were carefully taking fingerprints from every surface.

"Jane, I hope they clean up before they leave your house," Shelley said. "That black powder is making a mess. It's a good thing we had all the kids fingerprinted last year when they had the program at school. That way, you don't have to involve them any more than—Jane?"

"What?"

"I said—Jane, what's the matter with you?"

"I think I know. It was what Charlene said."

"Know what?"

"Everything. Why and who and even how!" She leaped up and ran after Mel. "Wait!" she shouted at him. "Come back. We have to talk!"

"All right, I'll admit you *could* be right," Mel said twenty minutes later.

"It all fits! What do you mean I 'could' be right?"

"It's all circumstantial, Jane."

"But the fingerprints in the kitchen will prove it, won't they?"

"The fingerprints will only prove that someone was in your kitchen. Not why or when or with what intent."

"But it's obvious! To find the tape and to pick up a handy weapon!"

"Jane, a trial lawyer would make mincemeat of that. He'd say his client just took an irrational, over-whelming dislike to you and trashed the kitchen as an expression of it. He'd say he was so sorry to have it brought out. It wasn't reasonable or nice to do, but still, we all do stupid, ugly things sometime in our lives and it doesn't make us murderers."

"Oh, Mel!" Jane felt like stamping her foot like a thwarted child. "Why are you countering everything I say?"

"Because I have to. If you can't even convince me a hundred-percent that this is the *only* possible explanation, how could I possibly convince a pros-ecutor to go to court with it? And if I don't know I can convince a prosecutor, I can't make an arrest. I don't dare!"

"Okay, okay. I see that. But Mel, just tell me unofficially, do you think I'm right?"

"I'm sure of it."

"So what are you going to do about it?"

"Everything I'm legally able to. Complete de-tailed questioning of all the suspects and wit-nesses, file a million reports, crawl over the evidence, look for new evidence to corrobo-rate this theory—and hope for some damned good luck."

*　　*　　*

Thelma was delighted at the prospect of having Katie and Todd spend the night with her. "I was going to call you anyway," she said. "I just saw on the noon news that that actress died practically in your yard. It's not a healthy environment for children."

Jane couldn't imagine how Thelma could have heard about Lynette's death, still officially assumed to be a suicide, without also hearing about Jake's very definite murder the day before, but she cast her eyes heavenward and whispered, "Thanks."

"What was that?"

"Nothing. I'll bring them straight from school then. And pick them up in the morning?"

"Oh, Jane. Leave them all day. I want to take them shopping. I noticed that Todd's jeans are looking a tiny bit worn." That was Thelma's euphemism for "shabby." Jane didn't bother to tell her mother-in-law that Todd worked very hard at getting them that way.

"Then I'll pick them up around four."

She got all their things together and headed out.

"Scott's got some little cousins visiting," Mike said when she got to the high school. "He promised to take them to the Museum of Science and Industry tomorrow, so it'll be an all-day thing. Give me my stuff and I'll just go home with him. Be back tomorrow for dinner unless I call first."

That was when a couple of very disparate, but interlocked plans started to take shape in Jane's mind.

"Mom, don't you think you ought to go stay someplace else? A hotel or something?"

She smiled. "I'll be fine. Really fine. Don't worry about me. But if you call home and I'm not there, it's just because I decided to do that. In fact—oh, there's Scott's car. Here's your stuff."

She checked that she had a credit card with her, made a couple of stops and smiled all the way home. She even smiled through a whole telephone conversation with Thelma. Then she went looking for Shelley to lay out her plan.

—— 25 ——

By seven o'clock much of the heavier equipment was gone. The props truck had been removed, as had the wardrobe trailer, the condor, the scenery trucks, and one of the electrical trucks. There were no cameras in sight, no microphones, and the heavy cables that once snaked all over the field had disappeared.

The wardrobe tent remained, however, and the center partition had been removed to make a large eating area. A dozen round tables and their chairs now filled the area and spilled out into the yard beyond. With the scenery flats gone and most of the big reflectors and the lighting equipment missing, the field behind the house was beginning to look like it did before the movie production company arrived.

Jane let the cats out to explore and put Willard in his dog run, where he could now bark his brains out if he wanted without disturbing the filming. Jane rescued her lawn chairs before they could be accidentally packed up and hauled away. According to her contract with the production company, by Monday evening everything would be gone and she and the neighbors would have new fences installed.

When she brought Willard back in, the catering truck was just arriving, as were some of the party attendees. The street in front of her house was starting to fill up with the cars of the extras and local crew members who were entitled to attend the wrap party and wanted to be there early to enjoy every minute of it.

But her plan, if it were to work at all, couldn't be executed until everyone had arrived. She took a long, soothing bath, washed her hair and took special care with drying and curling it, and put on a slinky peacock blue dress she'd bought to attend the theater on her weekend in New York with Mel. It was a remarkably flattering dress, which she wouldn't have even bothered to try on if Shelley hadn't insisted. Even on the hanger, she'd found the plunging neckline downright alarming. She had great shoes to go with it, but they were high heels and she couldn't walk around the yard in them without nailing herself into the ground, so she settled for some taupe flats that were decent enough as long as nobody looked too closely.

Shelley was just coming out of her house as Jane exited her kitchen door. "My God! You *do* clean up good!" Shelley exclaimed. "That dress is terrific! Mel will fall down drooling."

"I hope so. I keep expecting the ghost of my great-grandmother to show up shouting, 'Cover your chest, girl!' "

"Mel's going to be here tonight, isn't he?"

"Yes. I spoke to him this afternoon."

"You didn't tell him—"

"No, not all of it. Just that I had a couple things in mind that might help."

They strolled over to the catering truck where a line had already formed to partake of the wrap party dinner. Shelley studied the menu scrawled on the chalkboard hung from the end of the truck. "Oh, great! Tex-Mex. Jane, if you get near anything with sauce, I'll smack you. I couldn't stand for something to get spilled on that dress."

"I'm too nervous to eat anyway," Jane said. "May I have a drink? Maybe I could ask for it in one of those cups with a lid."

"Don't be fresh," Shelley said with a smile, using her mother's favorite phrase.

Jane and Shelley got soft drinks, although there was beer available, the first time they'd seen any alcohol on the set. They drifted about, seemingly aimlessly for a while, exchanging pleasantries with various people. Actually they were taking roll, waiting for everyone they needed to arrive.

There were a surprising number of people they had difficulty recognizing. Instead of being in costume, as they had been all week, the extras were dressed in party clothes with makeup and their real hairstyles. Many of them looked vastly different as themselves. Most of the partygoers were dressed casually, but a few, like Jane and Shelley, had put on their best.

Mel's reaction to Jane was highly satisfactory. "Wow!" he said, looking her up and down lecherously when he arrived. "You look fantastic!"

In all the years of her marriage, her husband had never said anything to her in quite that tone of voice. Jane felt herself blushing and had to suppress a girlish giggle that was forcing itself up her throat. "Thanks," she said, in a squeaky voice.

He stared at her a minute longer, then forced himself to say in a businesslike tone, "Now, about your call this afternoon—?"

"We just want to see if we can 'break the barrier' of secrecy. If it works, it'll be up to you to follow through."

"And if it doesn't, you'll have put yourselves in danger," Mel said.

"No, because there will be too many witnesses," Jane assured him. "Just sit down and look as inconspicuous as you can while Shelley and I gather people up."

"Where?" Mel asked, peering into the semidarkness of the tent.

"Over there." Jane tilted her head at the far corner where Olive Longabach had been sitting alone until Maisie took pity on her and sat down a moment before. "That table isn't going to fill up any time soon with Olive casting a pall of grief over it. Shelley, you join them and keep the table free, would you?"

When Shelley had gone, Mel leaned close to Jane and said, "I don't suppose I can stop you from doing this, can I?"

Jane shook her head.

"If my superiors had any idea I was going along with this crazy scheme—"

"You're not 'going along' with anything, Mel. You may, with luck, find yourself a fortunate accidental witness to a confession. That's all. And you may not," she added. "Go sit down and we'll see."

Jane found Butch and the props intern deep in conversation and butted into it. "Butch, could I speak to the two of you in a few minutes?"

"Sheesh! Jane! You look bitchin'," he exclaimed.

"I guess that's good? Thanks. I really need to talk to you guys. It'll only take a minute. Go to the table in the corner where Maisie is sitting. I'll be there in a sec."

Jane then extracted, with some difficulty, Angela Smith from a tête-à-tête with a handsome electrician and sent her to the table. It took her only a minute more to locate George Abington, who was standing in front of the catering truck, studying his options grimly. Grousing about the trendiness of the menu, he went compliantly.

Roberto Cavagnari was almost as easy.

"Could I have a few minutes of your time?" she asked him, putting her hand on his arm.

"Who *are* you?" he exclaimed dramatically, leering at her.

"The Spirit of Justice!" Jane responded theatrically.

As she hoped, this caught his interest. That, and (she suspected) her cleavage, seemed enough to get his attention for a moment. Which was all she needed.

She led him into the cavern of the tent, steering him through the tables to where the rest had gathered.

"How nice of you all to join us," Maisie said, looking perplexed. "I was just telling Olive—" her voice trailed off as she looked around the table.

Nobody was listening to her. They were all looking expectantly at Jane.

"I want to ask you all a few questions," Jane said. She glanced around and didn't see Mel. He'd hidden himself a little too well for her liking. But she noticed one of the other police officers, out of uniform and, likewise, almost unrecognizable, at the adjoining table.

"Yeah?" Butch asked. "What kinda questions?"

Jane leaned on the back of a chair to help steady herself. Her knees were shaking. What if she'd come this far and was utterly wrong and about to make a prize ass of herself? "Maisie? You told me something interesting the first day of work here."

Maisie looked startled. "I did?"

"You said Lynette Harwell had been on sets that had bad luck. Remember? Tell me again what kind of bad luck you mentioned."

"I—I don't know—uh, accidents, injuries of various kinds, illnesses—"

"—and thefts, you said."

"Yes, I guess I did."

"Important thefts?"

Maisie shrugged. "I don't know."

Roberto was deep in thought. He muttered to himself for a few minutes and said, "Yes. I heard—"

"What did you hear?" Jane prodded.

"Lynette's last film. Before this one. There was talk of a man who almost died because his medicine was taken from the set. I do not know what the illness was, but the pills were important to him."

Jane nodded. "And on this set, too, there were thefts. Mr. Cavagnari's watch—"

"No, no, no. This was not stolen," Roberto said. "This I misplaced among the food."

"But Jake had looked on that table only minutes before and he didn't see it there," Jane said. "Is that likely?"

"Impossible!" Butch said. "Jake couldn't miss seeing something he was lookin' for if it was right in front of his eyes. Anybody else could, but not Jake."

"So whoever stole it must have put it there," Jane said. "Just as whoever stole the cash put it in the cup in the makeup trailer?"

"Jokes! You mean these were jokes?" Cavagnari said. "This is not a thing of good taste to do!"

"Oh, they weren't jokes," Jane assured him. "And I misspoke a moment ago when I said the person who stole the things put them back. Butch's medallion and Angela's ring were also stolen, but there wasn't time to put them back. Was there?"

She looked slowly around the table, meeting the eyes of each person in turn.

"Was there, Olive?" she finally said softly.

—— 26 ——

A babble of conversation broke out and Butch's voice finally cut through it. "You mean Olive stole that stuff?"

"No, Olive didn't steal things. Olive returned them," Jane said.

Olive had started to rise, but Shelley was standing behind her and had laid a firm, but gentle, hand on her shoulder.

"You see, Lynette Harwell was a kleptomaniac," Jane said. "That's probably what she was treated for at the psychiatric hospital. Not substance abuse like everyone assumed. And what Mr. Cavagnari said about her last film before this probably explains why. My guess is that the medicine the man needed to take was very likely in an attractive container. A container Lynette stole. When Olive Longabach realized how close her mistress had come to killing someone, she persuaded her to get help. Or perhaps forced her to get help. Is that right, Olive?"

The older woman sat with her head down, staring at the table, and didn't respond.

"But it didn't work. The treatment didn't stick. In fact, she might have been worse than ever. The watch, the ring, the money, the religious medallion. Olive was being run ragged trying to keep track of the things Lynette was lifting whenever she got a chance. That's what Jake realized and it led to his death. He had a phenomenal memory for objects. He *knew* the watch wasn't on the table when he looked for it. A moment later, after Olive had been there getting tea for Lynette, the watch appeared. To someone with a suspicious mind like his, it didn't take any more to make him realize what had happened."

"How did he know Olive hadn't stolen it herself?" Maisie asked Jane the question, but was looking at Olive, who still had not acknowledged the conversation.

"We'll never know," Jane said. "Maybe it was a lucky guess on his part. But he knew all the gossip in the business and maybe he put together some information we don't have to come to the conclusion that it was Lynette, not Olive."

"Speaking of lucky guesses, isn't that what you're doing?" George Abington said. He hadn't spoken before and his voice now was tired.

"No, we have a film record of him trying to blackmail Lynette into helping Angela get the vacant role. Remember? The public relations man who taped the lunch? Jake had been hand signing to Lynette, telling her he knew that she was a kleptomaniac. I took the film home to throw it away, but I had—I had other things on my mind and I ended up accidentally keeping it. That's why my kitchen was vandalized. Lynette probably didn't understand signing, but Olive did."

"I'm sorry, Jane, but this doesn't make sense," George Abington said. "Kleptomania? That's just a mental illness. Not a very attractive or appealing one, I'll admit, but—"

"Didn't you know, George?" Jane asked him.

He didn't answer for a long moment, then he sighed and said, "I suspected. We were married only a very short time and my life was in a turmoil for the duration, but things did keep disappearing and turning up someplace else. I tried to talk to Olive about it, but she acted so offended that I backed off. Then Roberto came along and it didn't matter to me anymore."

Olive had looked up for a minute while he spoke and gazed at him sadly, but then she went back to studying her hands in her lap.

Talk, Olive! Jane thought frantically. *It doesn't mean anything unless you talk.* She heard someone behind her clear his throat and she glanced back to see Mel. He nodded his encouragement.

"But it mattered to Olive," Jane said. "Olive knew that taking drugs or having affairs or fighting with the I.R.S. were acceptable foibles in the publicity mill. But kleptomania? No, Lynette would have been a figure of fun for that. It isn't, as George says, a very sympathetic ailment or one that most people can identify with. There would have been jokes, suspicion, maybe even arrests, if she'd pinched something valuable and gotten caught with it."

Shelley was gently patting Olive's shoulder now.

"More important," Jane went on, "Lynette might steal something that did someone genuine harm. She almost did when she took somebody's medicine."

"It was in a gold box. A gold pillbox . . ." Olive said in a near whisper.

It isn't a confession, but it's a step in the right direction, Jane thought. She felt Mel's hand, warm, on the back of her waist.

"So Olive had to silence Jake," Jane went on. "She knew that George suspected the truth, but she also knew he was a good man who wouldn't gossip. But Jake was a different matter, wasn't he, Olive?"

No response.

"Jake had to be silenced before he could tell everybody. And then fate intervened." Jane could have bitten her tongue for saying something so trite, but she had the rapt attention of her small audience and plunged on. "The next day Lynette gave the performance of her life. A performance that would be a classic, that would save and enshrine her reputation. And not only was it a superb performance, it was the last scene of the movie that she was in. It was the perfect time to save her from herself. That's what you did, wasn't it Olive? You saved her from ruining her reputation. You locked her in amber at her peak."

Jane stopped speaking and waited. The silence around the table was as real as a block of ice with them all frozen into its cold grip. Those at the adjoining tables, sensing the tension, had grown quiet, too.

Finally Olive looked at Jane. And nodded. "Jake was an awful person," she said hesitantly. "He didn't care who he hurt. Poor Lynette couldn't help herself, but he'd have talked about her. People would have laughed at her. And now *you've* told everyone. You are a wicked young woman."

Jane stiffened with outrage. This woman had killed two people in cold blood and called Jane wicked? But she managed to keep her voice calm and soothing. "Why now, Olive? You watched over her all her life. Why did you have to kill her? You made her get professional help once. You could have done it again. And eventually it would have worked. She would have been cured in time."

"But I won't be," Olive said.

"You're ill?" Maisie asked her.

Olive nodded. "Cancer," she said bluntly.

This stunned everyone but Shelley into silence. Shelley asked, "How did you get her to drink the tea, Olive? It must have tasted awful."

Olive looked up at Shelley, her chin quivering. "I told her it was something good for her. She drank it."

Jane's voice was trembling with anger and sadness. "All we ever saw was Lynette bossing Olive around, but it was really Olive who pulled the strings. Olive told her how to dress, did her makeup, even found the book this movie was based on and persuaded Lynette that it would be a good role for her. Lynette couldn't have found her way out of a closet without Olive showing her where the door was. You wrote the note the limo driver was given, didn't you, Olive?"

Olive nodded.

"And you dressed her and did her hair?" Jane continued.

"I told her some photographers were coming," Olive said in a weary, sad tone. "She was getting sleepy, so I told her to just rest for a bit and I'd wake her when they arrived. It had to be that way. I couldn't have her found in disarray."

Mel and the other officer had gotten up and moved quietly to each side of her. Shelley stepped back and Mel leaned down to speak to Olive. "I think you should come with us, Miss Longabach, and tell us all about it."

Olive shrugged as if it didn't matter anymore. "Now everyone knows. It was a waste. Poor little Lynette." She reached into her handbag and took out a handkerchief, which she dabbed at her eyes with before rising. Very calmly and with great dignity, she took the arm of the other officer and let him lead her from the tent.

It was almost ten when Mel returned to Jane's house. She was still in her fancy dress, watching an old movie on television. A local television station, in honor of Lynette's death, was rerunning her first starring film.

Mel came into the living room and sat down beside Jane on the couch. "She was good, wasn't she?" he said.

"She was a wonderful actress. Sometimes. I talked to the others at the table after you left. They all swore to keep the kleptomania a secret if possible. Who knows if they will?"

Mel put his arm around her. "It won't have to come out in a trial. Olive has confessed. Poor old thing. I don't think she has any idea of what she's really done."

"She was as single-minded as Lynette," Jane said.

"Jane, you did a good thing tonight."

"I don't feel like it."

She got up and pushed the button on the television to turn it off and forced herself to shake the mood and smile. "What are you doing now?"

"I just wanted to check in with you and I didn't feel like phoning. You look gorgeous. Have I mentioned that?"

"I don't mind hearing it as many times as you care to mention it. Do you have to go back to your office?"

"For about an hour. Why?"

Jane went to the end table where she'd put her purse. Opening it, she took out two white plastic cards about the size of credit cards with an arrangement of round holes punched through. "Todd and Katie are staying with their grandmother tonight and Mike is at his friend Scott's," she said conversationally as she handed one of the plastic cards to Mel.

"What's this?"

"What does it look like?"

"One of those electronic hotel keys. What have these got to do with the case?"

Jane smiled as she walked over and picked up a small overnight case sitting by the window. "I'm happy to say they have absolutely nothing to do with the murders, Mel. They're keys to the room where I'm staying tonight. I checked in this afternoon. Maybe you'd like to drop by later . . . ?"

He stood up and took the overnight case from her. "Janey, it would take a fire, a flood, and half a dozen more murders to keep me away."

Nationally Bestselling Author

J·A·JANCE

The J.P. Beaumont Mysteries